CONVENIENT PREY

A NOVEL

AV IAIN

ELENA

11.31 AM, SATURDAY

Elena Kardos gently cradled her baby's head against her shoulder and stared at the unlit electric fireplace in her mother's front room. A tremor passed through her but not because it was cold. On the contrary, it was an unseasonably warm September morning. No, the tremor was the feeling she got whenever she realised she was alone.

She lost herself in her baby's even respiration, the warmth from his breath seeping through her blouse. It brought goose pimples rising up from her skin. Every day he seemed to grow a little heavier. Every day he became less of a baby, and more of a human being. She slipped a glance at him as he slept, the side of his head resting upon the cloth which draped over her shoulder.

George.

That was his name.

It was difficult to think of him by name. It made it seem like he was more grown up than he actually was. It reminded her that he would one day leave her behind.

Go about his own life.

Somewhere off in the house — her *mother's* house — she heard something fall.

She startled.

Her heart beat up in her throat.

And her pulse quickened.

A hot flush settled in over her cheeks.

George stirred in her arms, opening his huge, dark-blue eyes, blinking at his surroundings before, smacking his lips lazily, drifting back to sleep.

Although it was clearly something which had been poorly placed falling of its own free will — of *gravity's* will — Elena continued to stare in the direction of the sound for the best part of a minute.

Her mother had gone to the corner shop.

And Elena was all too aware that she was alone in the house.

She suppressed her fear.

It was *her* problem.

That was the reason why he had left.

Because she had been needy.

Because she had wanted to be close to him all the time.

Because she had wanted *him* to keep her safe.

But, well ... that was the past now.

She and George had been living at her mother's for the better part of a year. When her best friend would ask her, with an arched eyebrow, how she could possibly stand living under the same roof as her mother — especially now that she had a child — Elena found herself forced to play up to the stereotype; to claim that she was wilting under a barrage of criticism, that she *was* looking for some-where else. That this was only a temporary situation. That she *would* have some "space" for herself soon.

But, to tell the truth, she was more than happy here.

Her mother was a pensioner. She hardly left the house. And since Elena hardly left the house either it meant that neither of them was ever alone.

Well, *almost* never.

When Elena heard the footsteps crunching up the tidy gravel driveway, the *scrub* of the key in the lock, it was like a weight had lifted off her shoulders.

All at once the hot flush, the hollow feeling left her.

She felt a cooling, calming sensation pass through her bloodstream. From where she stood in the sitting room, she turned her head in the direction of the front hall.

The door opened and shut.

There was an exhalation.

Her mother appeared in the sitting room doorway.

She wore a winter jacket despite the warm weather. Elena had often joked that her mother had an equatorial condition. Her mother clasped the local newspaper — *The Goonherth Bay Chronicle* — beneath her arm. Elena could just about make out the headline: "Indian Summer Boils The Bay".

Some people thought it was depressing to end up living in the same place where you grew up. When she'd been at school others had often spoken about "getting away" or "escaping Goonie".

Everyone wanted to leave.

Everyone wanted to stride out into the Big Bad World.

To see what it was all really about.

What *they* were really all about.

Well, Elena *had* been out into the Big Bad World and it had chewed her up, spat her out, left her here, where she had started.

At thirty-six now, in the year she had been home, Elena had got to wondering if she wasn't where she was supposed to be all along.

"Feels like it's all about to break out there," her mother said, speaking in her native Hungarian. She glanced to George, snoring away on Elena's shoulder, and then she padded toward the kitchen. "A storm later this evening, believe me."

When Elena replied, she spoke in English. She had never really got into the habit of speaking Hungarian back to her mother, knowing that she understood English just as well. "I'll put George down," she said. "Make us a cup of tea."

Her mother made no response.

As usual, her mother seemed to be off in a world of her own. She muttered to herself as she rustled about with the plastic bags in the kitchen, putting things into their place. Her mother had always taken great pride in keeping things organised — in making sure that her home wasn't only spotless but *tidy* too.

Elena had never been good at that sort of thing. She just tended to spread everything out. Allow piles to accumulate. To only deal with things when it became obvious that there was nothing else to be done. That everything would fall down about her ears if she neglected to do *something* right at that moment.

Elena trudged up the narrow staircase, taking care with where she put her feet. It was a recurring nightmare of hers that she would lose her footing and tumble, falling at the foot of the steps, crushing George beneath her. Of course she knew this to be a somewhat *wild* fantasy given that she was hardly the *heaviest* of women. Indeed, she weighed only a shade over fifty kilos; something the doctor had tut-tutted about at her last appointment. And then there was the fact that she simply took so much care with George — that because her every waking thought was devoted to him — it was extremely unlikely that he would come to harm while in her care.

She laid George down in her bedroom, in the travel cot by the window.

It was bizarre to still think of it as "her" bedroom. It seemed that the day she'd left home her mother had taken a bin liner to every last thing Elena had left behind.

Gone were all the stuffed toys of her youth.

Posters too.

Neither was there any trace of the small, elegantly crafted guitar which her father had given her for her sixth or seventh birthday ... shortly before he had been "lost at sea", as her mother euphemistically put it.

"Her" bedroom was really now nothing more than a guest room, what with its neutral, cream-coloured linen, and the lack of anything other than the bedside table and lamp, the opened suitcase in the corner, the cot standing by the window.

Elena no longer bore a grudge. Maybe when she'd been younger.

In her twenties.

But not now.

When she had left her mother's house behind, fifteen or so years ago, she hadn't looked back. And she had hardly returned to visit.

It wasn't as if her mother inhabited a mansion either. It was a simple, two-bedroom, semi-detached with a boxy back garden. The only thing the house really had going for it was the sea view.

The view down on Goonherth Bay.

Elena lost herself in the sparkle coming off the water. It was hard to believe that winter was on its way. That in a month or so she would have to wear a jumper indoors and out. Her mother would dig out her thermal underwear from the attic. Perhaps she would throw another coat on top too.

It was strange to think that this was, perhaps, the best Elena had felt in months. And yet, even a year before, it would've escaped her to believe that right now she might be standing in her former bedroom, looking out the window, nearing the middle of a lazy Saturday morning.

But this was where life had left her.

She glanced down to George, taking in his doll-like face another time. She was about to leave the room behind when something out of the window caught her eye.

A battered estate car. Hardly a remarkable sight. Dozens of them trundled down the cobblestones of Pwelbock Street, headed for the beach, every day.

Apart from the driver, the car was unoccupied.

No children in the back seat.

No wife sat up front.

And, the final detail, no dog in the boot.

Elena stared. Had she matured into one of those "curtain twitchers" she had sworn in her teenage years she'd never become? She blinked a couple of times, hoping to break her concentration. To get shot of her auto-hypnosis.

Then her pragmatic mind kicked in.

Three, four times a year there was a suicide in the Bay.

Someone leaping off the cliffs and into the thrashing waves of the Atlantic below.

Everyone along the coastal roads recognised the red flags.

Solitary males aged between eighteen and forty.

She got a brief glimpse of the face through the tinted glass of the windscreen:

Curly blond hair.

Cherubic cheeks.

Rich hazel eyes.

She blinked.

The fog of memory lifted.

She recognised the face.

She *knew* who it was.

And although recognition flickered through her mind, she couldn't quite bring herself to recall the name right away. A mental block ... until there was nothing *but* the name:

Henry.

Harry.

Harry Foldes.

The car turned the corner, heading off along a narrow side passage which skirted the coast and which led to The Crosses ... the Foldes' family home. When the car had slipped completely from view, Elena continued to stare into the space left behind.

The warbling grey-green sea a blurry backdrop.

In all the time since she had been back she hadn't seen him once.

Like everyone else he had moved away ... or so she'd heard.

Was he back to visit?

Her mother called from downstairs.

Elena stared out of the window for another few seconds and then turned.

With a final glance at George — snoring away lightly in his travel cot — she slipped from the room. As she made her way down the stairs, Harry Foldes's face remained emblazoned upon her mind's eye.

She had thought it was all done with.

... Well, it was ... but of course Goonherth Bay was *his* home too.

His family was here.

Why should she have thought anything else?

When she reached the bottom of the staircase, she noticed she was trembling. It took her another few seconds — three, four deep breaths — to regain her composure.

She would be fine.

That was what she told herself.

She would be fine.

She was safe ... wasn't she?

————

Back downstairs, in the kitchen, Elena was in shock.

On her way down the stairs, she had slipped twice.

There had been a heart-stopping moment when she had dangled on the very edge of one of the steps, believed that her hold on the banister would give way, and that she would tumble down. Land sprawled in the front hall.

Break her neck.

But she'd held her balance.

Somehow defied physics.

She breathed in the thick steam as it plumed from the large metal saucepan on the stove. Her mother was making hortobágyi palacsinta, a crêpe stuffed with veal. She breathed in the thick scent of the frying onions mingled with spices. A bowl of chopped parsley sat on the kitchen counter ready to sprinkle on top when the dish was served. It was almost lunchtime and hortobágyi palacsinta was one of Elena's all-time favourite dishes. So why wasn't she more excited?

Why didn't she feel any hunger?

Still dressed in her thick winter's coat, her mother turned to her. She gave Elena one of those wizened looks which suggested she could read her mind. Her mother always claimed she had gypsy blood. "You need your strength," she said, and then, shaking her head as she turned back to languidly stir the pot, "You need to eat more. Nothing but skin and bones. You need strong milk. For your baby. For Georgie."

Elena felt herself blush. It wasn't because of what her mother had said. Or that she might somehow be malnourishing George with her deficient breast milk. It was because Henry Foldes annoyingly still lingered on her mind.

Henry *Fucking* Foldes.

Glancing to the table, seeing that the cutlery had not yet been placed, Elena busied herself gathering up knives and forks and spoons. She noticed there were no paper napkins left in the packet and so slipped into what they fancifully referred to as the "pantry".

The "pantry" wasn't much more expansive than a broom cupboard.

The plastic packet of napkins was on the top shelf.

Elena kicked the wooden footstool into place and clambered on top, steadying herself against the shelves. Even on the stool, she could only just brush the packet of napkins with her fingertips. It was a wonder her mother had managed to place them so far out of reach. Elena was a good inch or so taller. With a final swipe, Elena knocked the packet off the shelf and onto the floor. While she stooped to recover the napkins, however, she noticed two cans of tinned tomatoes also lying there. She supposed that was what she had heard falling while her mother had been out.

There was something else too.

Something beneath them.

A letter.

Elena pictured the scene in her mind. That the letter had been slotted between the cans before they had taken a tumble. She imagined the cans balancing precariously on the edge of the shelf until — one day, today — the rumble of a passing lorry had been enough to send them falling.

She picked the letter up.

It was addressed to her:

Ms Elena Kardos

She saw it had come via her old address. She had had a postal redirect service set up so she would get her post here, at her mother's house.

She scanned the postmark.

That was strange.

It was dated from two months ago.

Even allowing for the redirect that was a long delay. And then there was the question of just what the letter was doing in the pantry ... not on the doormat, where letters traditionally entered the household ...

With a dozen questions on her mind, Elena picked her way out of the pantry and back into the kitchen. "Mum?" Elena said. "What's this?"

"Hmm?" her mother said, turning away from the stove.

Her eyes fell upon the envelope.

A look of concern crossed her face. She met Elena's gaze.

Elena turned her attention back to the letter. Her hands were trembling as she turned it over in her hands. She saw a familiar crest stamped onto the back. She recognised the cursive writing immediately:

Saint Camelgal High School.

Her old school.

She slipped her fingernail beneath the flap and gently tore it open.

She slipped out and unfolded the letter within.

She scanned the first paragraph, the greeting, the well-wishing, shifted to the next few sentences. It was an invitation.

An invitation to a school reunion.

She retraced the words she'd already read through, absorbing them properly for the first time:

A twentieth anniversary.

It struck Elena in the chest, almost like a physical blow.

Had it *really* been twenty years?

She was thirty-six now ... so, well, it made sense.

At least on a logical level.

But why would logic ever be concerned with memory?

She glanced up from the letter, realising her mother was still watching her with extreme expectation. A flash of rage passed through Elena's veins. "Why did you hide this?" she asked, spontaneously breaking into Hungarian.

Her mother, apparently equally taken back by Elena's Hungarian as the letter she had discovered, retreated a few steps from the large pot. Her arms fell to her sides, the ladle she still held steaming and dripping onto the floor.

"Mum?" Elena said, taking a step toward her. "Tell me the truth."

Her mother didn't back away any further. She stood her ground.

And she met Elena's eyes.

But said nothing more.

Elena looked to the letter again. There was a slip she was supposed to fill out and return ... *RSVP*. Eyes fixed once more on the page, she addressed her mother.

In English this time.

Her voice croaked as she spoke.

"Why?"

Her mother still didn't reply.

Was she concerned Elena might become violent?

That she might lose her head?

There was no basis for her mother to believe so. It was a rare occasion when Elena would raise her voice and she had never — in all her life — physically assaulted anyone.

Which was more than George's father could say ...

She held herself still, feeling the anger continuing to drip through her. At the same time, however, a sense of perspective slowly began to dawn. It was obvious. Her mother didn't need to say anything. She had only wanted to protect her.

Just as Elena protected George.

It was *only* natural.

Elena calmed herself, continuing to hold the letter.

Finally, her mother spoke. This time in English.

"It is not too late," she said.

Elena absentmindedly examined the letter again.

The reunion would take place tomorrow.

Her mother was correct, of course. She *did* still have time.

But why would Elena ever want to go?

Her mother had done her a favour in keeping the letter from her.

And then a thought struck.

The reason — the reason *why* ... the reason why Henry Foldes was here.

Why he had come home.

A bolt up her back straightened her spine.

... *Fuck.*

She needed to warn them.

She needed to warn them *all*.

HENRY

11.50 AM, SATURDAY

Harry Foldes would've been the first to admit that his family mansion, The Crosses, was an overwhelming sight. Especially for anyone seeing it for the first time.

Indeed, even now, trundling his way up the sharply slanted gravel driveway, all the car windows rolled down, letting in the unseasonably warm autumnal seaside air, he felt skitters passing through his gut.

An almost paralysing squeeze over his abdomen.

He never enjoyed coming home.

Even at thirty-six he couldn't get over it.

Couldn't rationalise it.

"Home", as far as he could push that particular loaded term, was Goonherth Bay:

Good Old Goonie.

One of those hundreds of backwater places hidden away in the south-western reaches of the British Isles. Hours of driving from anywhere of import.

For Harry that meant London:

His City lifestyle.

His Islington penthouse.

His uncomplicated bachelordom.

He had grown so used to waking up with the sun rising on the London skyline. The Thames, the City skyscrapers, the Houses of Parliament, as he perused his wardrobe crammed full of designer suits. He worked as a hedge fund manager at Willats and Dodgely. Or, as it was colloquially referred to in afterhours by staff — and Henry was chief among them — Wallets and Dosh.

This morning, a Saturday, he had woken up so early he hadn't even had the chance to take in the sunrise. He had checked his phone.

Seen the "unfortunate" message.

And he had considered his options.

In the efficient manner of decision making which'd earned him millions in the past decade, he had taken a quick shower in an effort to cleanse himself of the whiff of champagne and women's perfume, and then donned a pair of jeans with a plain white t-shirt. The brown leather jacket thrown over his shoulders had completed the fifties style he was aiming for. Or so he'd hoped.

Then he had grabbed his overnight bag as he had prodded his feet into a pair of trainers he had once used for squash, but which had now been relegated to purely recreational use. The overnight bag was a small, hard-shelled suitcase on wheels. He kept the ready-packed suitcase concealed in his wardrobe for any short-notice business trips he might be required to attend.

Next, he had descended to the underground car park where his gaze had lingered longingly over his jet-black Maserati convertible before eventually firing up the sensible, second-hand Subaru estate he kept for homelier outings.

For when he expected a high probability of dings to the bodywork.

Normally when families, small children, were involved.

Whenever he came "home" it seemed that his car always bore the brunt of the harsh sea air. The uneven road surfaces. In more introspective moments he wondered if the dents and dings inflicted upon his car were a physical manifestation of the inner turmoil he suffered during each one of these "visits" home. And this particular visit home, he was sure, would be no different in terms of turmoil suffered.

As always, the problem which had summoned him home had started with a dismal chime from his personal mobile phone. He had specifically chosen a downbeat signal for any messages or — God forbid — phone calls from family.

This particular communication had come in the form of a text message from his father, preceded by two voicemail messages. Once Harry had seen the text message there was no need for him to waste time wading through voicemail.

It was a simple enough idea.

His mother was unwell — deathly so — and he was expected home.

As soon as possible.

As Harry had pulled onto the M4, the motorway which ran east to west and which — on more than one occasion — he had dubbed his own personal "Yellow Brick Road", he had felt that strangely nostalgic sensation grip him. That one which spoke to him of those stickiest of words: "family" and "home" … It was enough to make him pull off at the first service station and throw back a shot of something or other.

Get his mind straight.

But he didn't do that.

At work, he had seen enough careers brought to an abrupt halt by the inability to control emotions. From the inability to steer clear of temptation. Whatever else he was, Harry was a man now, and it was up to him to face up to things — to face up to life — without all of those little "helpers'" which only ever, in the end, got in the way.

In fact, Harry had just kept on going — no stops at all.

And he had ended up making the trip in a little under five hours.

As he crunched to a halt in front of The Crosses, dragging up the handbrake, he had crossed into another world entirely.

Gone was the hustle and bustle, gone was the constant trundle of traffic, the pedestrians marching along pavements. Gone were the greys, and the dirty whites, and the stodgy browns. A whole new palate greeted him now that he'd arrived "home".

Autumn was well on the way, of course.

He had taken in the yellows and the reds of the elm trees lining the driveway, fallen leaves carpeting the gravel. And then there was the perfectly manicured lawn. The bandstand at the bottom of the garden. Then, of course, encompassing and dominating everything, there was the view out over Goonherth Bay.

As Harry slipped out of the car, allowing the door to slam shut behind him, he took in the sparkle of the midday sun off the murky grey Atlantic.

For a couple of moments, he stood and stared across the waters, allowing the blazing blue skies to swallow him whole. He recalled, back when he'd been a kid, when he would steal out in the middle of a cloudless summer night, lie on the grass alone. He would tuck his hands behind his head and stare up into the twinkling, never-ending stars above. In those moments it felt almost as if the world moved around him.

As if he was at the exact centre of the universe.

He'd been more innocent back then.

More deluded.

Finally, realising he couldn't put it off any longer, Harry turned his attention to The Crosses itself. The house which, at least technically speaking, had been his childhood home. Although how anyone could ever call a house such as this one — a sprawling mansion — anything other than a "museum piece" escaped Harry completely.

The Crosses had the look of a countryside substance abuse clinic or some sort of high-end mental institution. The mansard roof produced this effect. As did the slender windows which never allowed more than meek slivers of daylight inside.

On instinct, Harry's attention shifted to the west wing, second storey.

To the room perched precariously on the corner.

What was — and what would always be — his bedroom.

Despite the fact he hadn't spent more than the occasional night there since his eighteenth birthday. Since he had gone to university and left all of this behind.

The house itself was constructed from cobblestone blocks, and Harry had often been brought in mind of a medieval castle when they would arrive at night here.

He recalled, back when he had been much younger, he had worried about the place being haunted. There was something about cobblestone which absorbed light.

Which seemed to bleed darkness.

And then there was the odd odour which always struck Harry when he had been away from The Crosses for a while, but which just as quickly became part of him again so that he didn't notice. There were days when he took it for the stench of rancid flesh, and then there were others when he dropped the melodrama and decided it was much closer to the scent of aged leather. Every room of the mansion had a fireplace, or at the very least a wood-burning stove, and so Harry had always felt that scent of ash clinging to everything. Constantly nagging at the back of his throat.

Choking him.

As he climbed the steps to the front door, a gull cackled over his shoulder.

He stood still, steadied himself.

He breathed in deeply.

He had always hated that fishy stink of the sea.

And he would've preferred to be anywhere else than here.

But here he was ...

He reached for the brass knocker, brought it down with a firm pair of thuds.

———

His father's smile went no further than his mouth.

As Harry clenched his hand, he noticed the drawn-out expression fixed in his father's eyes. The expression which spoke of sleepless nights; of stress mounting upon him. Almost impossible to bear. "Thank you for coming, son," his father said, his fingers now having gone slack and slipping free of the handshake.

Harry sniffed to himself — nothing more than a visceral reaction to coming "home" — and then he followed on his father's slippered heels. "Mum?"

His father blinked several times. Harry wondered if a tear might sneak free of his father's eyes, but he soon realised that his father wore an expression of someone who had already cried themselves dry. He had nothing left to give.

Not for the time being.

"Later," he said.

They had almost made it through the front hall when his father paused for a moment. As he often did when he was at home, his father wore a dressing gown over an ironed white shirt and a pair of dress trousers. When Harry had asked him about his dress once, his father had told him that it was to keep out the chill ... to save on central heating. Harry supposed that, if what his father said had any note of truth to it, then it was out of an environmental concern rather than an economic one.

His father would never need to worry for money.

Harry had always had the belief that his father donned the dressing gown as if he was some kind of boxer. As if he was just waiting for the signal to call him back into the ring — back to the *stage* — and he would allow the robe to fall away. And he would sit himself down once again on the piano stool.

Prepared to play.

His father dug into the inside pocket of the dressing gown, and produced, from within, a slightly crumpled envelope. "Almost forgot about this," he said, with a slight smile, handing the envelope over to him.

Harry took the envelope, turned it over in his hands, and then, seeing no notable features — no giveaway detail which might provide a clue to its origin or purpose — he stuffed it into his own pocket.

His father led him through the hallways. That familiar, musky smell continued to follow his father, the one which would be just as easily forgotten the moment that Harry left his company. When they reached the doorway to the Music Room, Harry paused for a moment to peer within.

His father's grand piano.

It shone in the sunlight which flooded in through the windows and off the bay.

It was the piano with which his father had performed so many concerts.

The one with which he had made so many recordings.

The piano which had paid for this home — for The Crosses.

Harry looked through the Music Room, past the many framed concert posters on the walls, and then out through the windows, to the garden.

"Got here just in time for lunch."

Harry turned away from the Music Room, catching his father's eye once again.

From somewhere he managed to summon a smile.

"Just how I planned it," he said.

There was an uneasy moment's pause between the two of them.

Finally, his father gave a nervous smile then an overly elegant flourish of his arm to indicate the corridor. That Harry should follow him.

And leave the Music Room behind.

With only a quick glance back over his shoulder, Harry caught sight of the pages of handwritten musical notation on the grand piano's music stand. He squinted at it for a moment. Was this some new masterpiece?

"It's getting cold," his father said.

Finally, Harry gave up trying to decipher anything of his father's scrawled notation and turned to leave.

As always, lunch was served in the kitchen.

All meals at The Crosses were served in the kitchen unless there was some special occasion. Birthdays. Christmases. It was a long — *long* — time since his father had hosted any sort of party. Not since Harry had been a child, perhaps twelve or thirteen. His father was the poster child of the brilliant recluse. Perhaps the greatest classical pianist of his era ... and he was living ... *here*.

In the middle of nowhere.

It had only occurred to Harry that it was an odd arrangement when he had run into musicians working in London; often playing a private gig in the City. Whenever Harry would think to speak with them he would soon find out that they had dozens of upcoming events — as many events as there were *dates* ... travelling all the time.

His father, though, aside from a choice few times, had barely left The Crosses.

Not since Harry had been born, anyway.

To begin with, when Harry had finally become conscious of his father's greatness, he had blamed it first on his mother, and then on himself.

Had his father given all of that up just so that he might have a quiet family life?

Feeling himself growing angry, Harry put the thought out of his mind.

He drew the kitchen in.

Unchanged, even after all these years.

Black marble work surfaces.

The Aga oven the colour of mulled wine.

And the homey, bare wooden floorboards, worn down by thousands of footsteps.

Harry couldn't help smiling.

He looked over to the Aga.

His father stood at the stove. He had peeled back the lid of an enormous metal pot. With a wooden spoon in hand, he was sipping at the contents.

Giving it a taste.

His father winced slightly.

"Inedible?" Harry asked.

His father glanced over at him, that ever-cheery expression sketched all across his face. "I'd hate to have to deprive my only child of a hot meal following a long journey just because he got cheeky."

Harry smirked. "What're you cooking there?"

"Leak and potato soup," his father replied.

It was funny to think that his father still spoke with a thick Cockney accent even after he'd lived so many years away from London. Then again, Harry supposed he had had so little company in the previous years that he'd hardly had the chance to lose or dilute it.

Harry inclined his head while his father set about the oven, pulling open one of the doors and producing a freshly baked loaf of bread from within. He watched as his father delicately sliced the warm bread, applying a smear of butter to each slice. When he brought over the bowl of steaming soup, accompanied by the plate of buttered bread slices, Harry felt as though he was famished. Once his father had set the bowl before him, it was all Harry could do to keep himself from bowing his head like a Labrador and lapping up its contents.

While Harry ate, his father eyed him watchfully, analysing each and every mouthful. As if he was attempting to garner feedback from each one of Harry's expressions.

"Dad?" Harry said.

"Hmm?"

"You're doing it again."

"Doing what ... oh ..."

His father backed away from Harry, his gaze no longer fixed so strongly upon him.

That was one of his father's habits. His attention to detail.

His *constant* desire for approval.

Were these the character qualities which'd pushed him to greatness?

Were these the same qualities which'd left him in his current state?

Which'd caused him to make the decisions he had made?

Once Harry got through with the soup, and feeling himself glowing from within, he straightened up in his chair. Almost despite himself, he felt a smile sneaking across his mouth. And he felt a tingle in the pit of his gut. Perhaps if Harry had allowed himself to speak from the heart — to the permit words to tumble free between his lips without first scanning them — something sentimental would've snuck out.

But, as it was, he waited for his blood to cool before speaking.

He allowed the smile to slip from his lips.

"Can I see her? Can I see Mum?"

———

The air in the east wing of The Crosses smelled strongly of ammonia.

A sinking feeling struck Harry.

He was suddenly deeply aware of his surroundings. Of the four-poster bed which his parents owned, and which they had owned throughout the entirety of their life as he remembered it. And of the walnut dresser. And of the matching walnut bedside tables, each of them bearing an ivory lamp with a sober shade the colour of sand.

The curtains were closed.

An oddly still quality hung over the room.

Harry felt his skin puckering up. His very bones seemed almost to resist his presence here. They appeared to want to push him away. To make him want to run.

He knew *that* feeling all too well.

He had experienced it during the early days of his career. The self-doubt which would attempt to sabotage his chances of closing the

Big Deal ... telling him that he wasn't good enough ... intelligent enough ... *talented* enough.

That he would get found out.

He had put those issues well behind him, though.

His bank account, if nothing else, was testament to that.

When Harry turned his attention back to the scene confronting him, he saw his mother lying propped up in bed. Her eyes were closed.

On the bedside table he made out a metal tray.

Glass vials, syringes.

Items the doctor had left behind following his latest visit.

When his father spoke, he startled him, appearing at his elbow without warning. "Wouldn't sleep all night," his father said. "Wanted to stay up and wait for you. Told her you most likely wouldn't make it till morning, of course, but she wouldn't listen to me. Just wanted to wait for you."

Harry had no idea what to say to this.

If his father was trying to make him feel bad for not dropping everything and coming at once — for not having paid *close* attention to his personal phone the previous evening — then he was going to be unsuccessful.

Harry had more than a decade of heavyweight therapy under his belt, and he was certain that he could manage just about any situation which might be thrown at him.

He had the techniques to manage any "crisis".

He was an expert at nipping such things in the bud.

"When did she fall asleep?" Harry asked.

"About two, three hours ago. Well before you arrived."

The stilted air hung heavy in the room.

Harry had the urge to throw open one of the windows, but he could tell, from his mother's pallid complexion, and from the way she wore blankets tucked all the way up to her chin, that this wasn't an option. He was afraid that a stiff breeze might cause her harm.

Because there was nothing else that he could do, he turned to his father again. "What did the doctor say?"

His father pouted. Hung his head. "It's just how I said it, Harry." He swallowed hard — a dry swallow which Harry thought he could almost *feel* himself.

"You mean ..." Harry turned back to his mother, looked over her, and then examined the tray of implements beside her.

"I wanted to choose the time," his father said. "A time when *you* were here." Tears glittered in his eyes. He tried to blink them away but without any effect. When he spoke again, his voice finally broke. He struggled to control his tone. "She's been in so much *pain* — you have to understand that."

Harry met his father's eye for the fraction of a second.

Then he looked back to his mother.

"You want ..."

"*Yes!*" his father broke in, not allowing Harry to finish. "It's been too long now — *too long* for her." He paused, and then spoke again, in a weaker voice, "It's been too long *for me*."

Although Harry had managed to keep a tight grip on his emotions throughout his time in his mother's presence, he lost it now. It was almost as if someone was attempting to wrench his heart clear out of his chest. A tear broke free of the corner of his eye. And then another. Before he could help himself, the tears ran in rivulets down his cheeks. He felt his father's firm hold on his shoulder.

"Come on, son," he said. "Let's have a drink."

ELENA

5.17 PM, SATURDAY

As if it would help to calm her nerves, Elena closed the curtains. She couldn't be one-hundred percent sure she had seen what she *had* seen. And yet she had believed enough to take action. She turned away from the window which looked onto Pwelbock Street and back into the sitting room of her mother's house.

She looked over those assembled before her.

It was so strange to see everyone again. To lay eyes on those familiar faces, all of them warped by the years but still carrying their obvious identifying features.

They were still the same people she'd gone to school with.

She looked over them in turn.

Jock Jones.

Back at school, he had worn his greasy black hair shoulder length. Now, though, it dragged down to his waist, tamed only by a single flaccid hair tie. He also wore a pair of sweatbands, one on each wrist. Each of these sweatbands had some sort of an emblem — a *logo?* — which Elena was unable to place. Judging from the rest of his appearance, she supposed it was some sort of druid rune.

It wouldn't surprise her.

Jock had always been in touch with *that* sort of thing.

She looked to the next.

Max Yardsman.

If Elena was being generous then she would say that Max weighed about 110 kg. Herself having only ever weighed over 60 kg while pregnant, she supposed she wasn't in any position to judge.

Max's head was shaved and he wore a polo shirt which seemed to be at least two sizes too small for him. Over the top he wore a smart-casual jacket. Underneath, he had on a pair of corduroy trousers which were a sort of sludge-green colour. Although she hadn't taken it upon herself to ask, she had noticed that he wasn't wearing a wedding ring. Neither was Jock.

Elena turned to the final member of the group.

Joanne Darkly.

Elena felt a smile creep onto her lips when she thought of Jock and Max's reaction when their eyes had drifted over Joanne. It had been a shock for them. How were they meant to know that one of the most popular girls at school had struck up a friendship with Elena in the past year. And that she was now — for want of a better term — Elena's *best friend*.

Joanne was a smouldering red head. Despite the two kids, the marriage — and *divorce* — she had gone through, she had seemingly held the same figure she'd had as a school girl. Her hair, too, was still luscious and full bodied, just as Elena's had become stringy and thinned after she'd had her child.

Joanne was proof — if ever it was needed — that life indeed *Wasn't Fair*.

At least when it came to appearances, anyway, because Elena had it on good authority, from personal confession, no less, that Joanne's life was anything but perfect.

That she had had *anything but* the life she deserved.

But, just as she had judged Max and Jock just now, she was certain that they would judge Joanne. Just as they had surely judged Elena herself.

Never having been the best at getting to the point, Elena looked to the mugs which everyone held, and said, in a mousy, downbeat voice which had somehow become her trademark, "Any more tea?"

Shakes of the head answered her question.

And she turned her thoughts back to the matter at hand.

To Henry Foldes.

Elena sort of floated across the room for several steps before finally descending on a nearby chair. She eased herself down but never got comfortable.

She remained perched on the edge.

Unable to quite commit herself to ... well, whatever it was that they were doing.

"I ... expect you're wondering why I brought you here tonight," Elena said, addressing Jock and Max mainly, but certain that Joanne's interest was just as piqued.

Elena drew a breath.

Took it down to her gut.

And then went on.

"Like me, you were all invited to the reunion — this weekend. *Tomorrow* afternoon."

A school reunion.

A twenty-year celebration.

Elena could still feel the squeezing sensation in her gut when she had got the letter through in the post. Her mother had known enough — that it would be nothing but a bad idea for her to go along. And then she had seen *him*.

Then she had seen Henry Foldes.

"I came back for it," Jock finally said.

"Me too," Max added.

Elena didn't need to put the same question to Joanne — the two of them *lived* in Goonherth.

Elena prepared herself, wondered if she couldn't hear George stirring upstairs. She wondered if she should just go up and check. This conversation *could* wait, after all.

... *No.*

She had to trust her instincts.

Although it shouldn't have been, it was clearly important to her.

Why else would she have called them all here together tonight?

"Henry Foldes is in town," she said, and then looked about their faces, hoping to see something ... hoping that she might *detect* something in their manner.

They exchanged glances.

Still said nothing.

Elena drew in another breath.

She was so tired of being afraid.

She was so *tired* of still feeling those echoes of what had happened all those years ago, back in school.

"You ... *remember*, don't you?" she said, addressing Max and Jock.

Neither one of them would meet her eye.

She realised that she was going to have to be blunter.

That she was going to have to *spell it out* to them.

"How he *bullied* you — the two of you?" She held herself still, not wanting to say anything further. It felt as if she had no other choice. "Remember what he did to *me*?"

Again, there was no response.

Elena held herself still. She could feel herself beginning to tremble all over. She couldn't quite believe she was doing this — that she was *doing* all this.

Over again.

From somewhere, she managed to summon the strength.

"Look," she said, "I brought you here tonight — I got in *touch* — because I thought that you might be interested in justice. Because you might want to have a chance to show Henry Foldes what he did. Show the *adult* Henry Foldes just what he was responsible for."

"Revenge?" Max pitched in, his chubby face creasing up.

Jock spoke next. "You're serious?"

Suddenly, Elena felt anything but. When the thought had occurred to her, it had seemed the most natural thing in the world —

that she should bring Max and Jock together so that they might have an opportunity to "get back" at Henry.

Perhaps she had gone a little crazy while she'd been here, while she'd returned to Goonherth.

Gone loony in Goonie, she thought to herself with a wry wit.

Goodness knew, there wasn't a lot else to do here.

Elena allowed her words to sink in with the two boys, and Jock finally found his voice.

"What did you have in mind?"

"I'm ... not sure," she replied.

"Just some sort of revenge?" Max put in, smiling openly now.

Elena couldn't say that she appreciated the snarky tone. She had brought the two of them here in good faith. She had wanted to help them.

Just as much as she had wanted to help herself.

She managed to hold her silence.

She could hear her mother clunking about with pots and pans in the kitchen. She wasn't a big fan of company and she wasn't shy of making her feelings known either.

"I thought we could work it out ... *between* us," Elena said.

It was then that Joanne yawned, then rose out of her chair, finding her feet. She shot Elena a what-the-hell-are-you-on glance and made for the front hall, and the door.

"Well," Joanne said, "guess you won't be needing me."

Elena couldn't help but notice how Max and Jock's gaze carefully followed Joanne across the room as if she was some sort of a goddess who'd recently taken on human form. Schoolboy infatuation was a powerful thing. Something which wasn't easily eroded even during the course of decades.

Before Joanne could leave the living room, however, Elena spoke up. "For what I've got in mind we'll *definitely* be needing you," she said.

Joanne stood still, as if physically pinned by invisible hands.

She pouted, then flipped a stray strand of hair over her shoulder.

Max and Jock were entranced by the gesture.

Joanne took a step back into the room. "And what will you be needing me *for*?"

"That depends," Elena said.

"*Depends* on what?"

"Whether or not you're committed."

Joanne scowled. "I don't follow — what's that *supposed* to mean?"

Elena met her stare, feeling nothing but resolve now.

Nothing but a steely determination.

"If you're on our side." She glanced to Jock and Max. "Or if you're on *his*."

Joanne remained where she was.

Unmoved.

And then she drew a deep breath, sighed it out, and took her seat.

JOANNE

6.45 PM, SATURDAY

With night-time draping itself across the landscape, Joanne cycled her way up the steep hill which led to The Crosses. The gravel driveway crunched beneath her bike tyres. She felt a tightness across her chest. Indeed, her whole body was rigid.

But it wasn't because of exertion from the bike ride.

When Elena had called her earlier that day, asked whether she would come over at once, Joanne had to admit she hadn't the faintest idea just what she might have in mind.

What the motive might be.

Joanne had thought it would be just for a chat.

For a cup of tea.

She was used to being Elena's confidante.

What she'd been through in the past year or so was despicable. How Elena's husband — had he been her husband, or simply the father of her child? — had treated her was nothing short of shocking. The things which Elena had told her.

The *violence*.

The *anger* ...

Joanne pushed down harder on the pedals, propelling herself up the hill, using her passionate reaction against Elena's ex-partner to drive her.

What was it about men?

Really, what *was* it?

How could there exist beings which, one moment, were like overgrown children, and then the next demi-godlike figures ... even if only in their own minds.

One thing was for certain, if Joanne had known that there was a chance of her having to cycle further than from her house to Elena's then she would've put on a more substantial layer of insulation than the threadbare denim jacket she currently wore.

She eyed The Crosses as it loomed above.

It reminded her of a monolith.

Was it the lack of lights?

Was it the sheer *size* of the place?

She recalled, back in school, when she had come to The Crosses for the first time — when Henry had invited one of her friends, and she had tagged along. She had had the same thoughts then when — as she did now — they had ridden their bikes up the driveway.

They had known everything about the Foldes, or, more accurately, they had known the same gossip which the entire town knew ... that Henry's father was a famous classical composer and pianist. And that he was a recluse. That, for some reason, unexplained, he had decided to hide away from the world. One thing had always struck her about Henry, and that was his reluctance to say even the most superficial of things about his family. As a topic of conversation his family had always been *Off Limits*.

Joanne had had enough of cycling up the hill after another minute or so.

She slipped out of the saddle, and walked alongside the bike, taking the handlebars to steer it up the slope. She could see that there was a single illuminated room in the mansion. One of the ground-floor rooms. The room which, she supposed, Henry currently occupied.

On instinct, she turned her gaze upward, to the upper floor.

To the room she knew to be Henry's bedroom.

Or the room which, once upon a time, *had* been Henry's bedroom.

When Joanne readied to approach the front door, and so to roll back the many years which lay between the two of them — since the last time they had seen one another — she couldn't help but think again on her task.

Think about just *what* she was doing here.

What she had been *sent* here to do.

Her instructions were simple.

First, she was supposed to make Henry aware of the school reunion if he wasn't already. Second, she was supposed to confirm his attendance there, so that the next part of the plan — whatever Elena believed it to be — could be put into place.

She saw the estate car parked in the driveway.

She knew this had to be *Henry's* car.

From what she had heard, he was living in London.

Had he driven down from there today?

It would make sense ...

As she readied to tread up to the front door, her attention was distracted by something off in the garden. Something ... *familiar*.

Leaving her bike propped up against the low wall which sheltered the flowerbeds at the front of the house, she went off to explore.

HENRY

6.59 PM, SATURDAY

Harry's father had led him down to the drawing room, where he kept his liquor cabinet. His father hadn't thought to ask him which drink he would prefer, without a word pouring out two tumblers of whisky. Just what sort of whisky it was Harry didn't bother to look. He took a slight interest in liquor and spirits but only because his clients were so often experts themselves. For Harry to know next to nothing about drinks would have exposed him as an outsider to them.

That he was *not* to be trusted.

Not to be trusted with their money ...

Now, though, he was very much Off-the-Clock.

Neither he nor his father had ever been a big drinker. In actual fact, the liquor cabinet itself was kept well stocked more out of respect for the craftsmanship of the furnishing itself than because of any appetite for alcohol.

In all of the tales which Harry had heard down the years about reclusive musicians — artists, and other sorts — there was almost always that same, repeated, boring element. The one which saw said artist losing themselves to a drug or drink addiction.

Often in the loneliest of circumstances.

For a while, in his twenties, Harry had wondered if his father might not be some sort of secret alcoholic, if he might not have been slugging back this or that on the sly. Not that his father's behaviour, or his abilities at the piano, would have shown any evidence for this theory. Then again, wasn't that part of being a "secret" alcoholic?

Wasn't part of the challenge in acting normally ... in functioning at a "high" level?

Although Harry didn't much believe in the idea of a photographic memory, he had always known that he possessed a certain talent for recollection. And he couldn't help but think to himself — as he looked over the drinks cabinet — that not one of those bottles appeared to have moved since his last visit over a year earlier.

Harry took a seat in one of the beaten-up armchairs which was positioned so as to look out through the windows into the garden, but also so as not to cut off the prospect of face-to-face contact with the rest of the drawing room.

The sun had already dipped in the sky.

Setting on the horizon.

Time here, in The Crosses, seemed to pass impossibly quickly.

Almost as if the pace of life itself sped up.

Perhaps it was because there was nothing for Harry to focus on — because there was nothing for him to *fix* his full attention onto. He had only to wander about the house. To stare out the window.

At the sea. In the moonlight.

Was this what his father did all day?

All *night*?

"She'll be eighty on Sunday," Harry's father said, out of nowhere, having taken a seat on the sofa across from Harry.

The sofa too looked out over the garden and Goonherth Bay.

Harry studied this for a moment.

He had always known his mother's birthday, of course.

There had been some sort of mental nag — at the back of his mind — for him to send something to her. He hadn't been planning on visiting, though. And, he supposed, on some subconscious level, he had believed, when he'd first picked up the phone and seen the message, that it might be his father imploring him to come home to "celebrate" his mother's birthday with them. His father had known that the only means of definitely bringing Harry back here was by upping the stakes.

By mentioning her approaching *death*.

What Harry *hadn't* known, however, was her exact age.

While Harry had been a child, it had been nothing but a juvenile curiosity which'd led him to nag his mother, asking her just *how old* she truly was. Later, though, into his twenties, he had better explained it to himself that adults — quite simply — didn't freely discuss their age ... for whatever reason believing it to be "rude".

Maybe it was something which he would better understand when he was older, if not wiser ...

" 'Eighty' ?" Harry echoed.

His father made a growling sound at the back of his throat.

Harry turned his attention back out the window, and over the garden, to the sea.

Eighty.

He supposed that was about right.

He had always known his father was younger than his mother.

But he had never *quite* known by just how much.

His father had recently turned sixty.

So his mother and father were twenty years apart.

Why this bothered Harry — if only for a moment — he couldn't quite say. When he turned to his father, he was all too ready to drop the whole subject. In the end, though, squeezing the tumbler of whisky in his hand, his father spoke of his own free will.

"She never wanted to speak about her age. Not with you. Not with *anyone*. She was always ... I don't know ... ashamed of the difference."

Harry eyed his father, tracing the wrinkles of his forehead around his eyes and then down his neck. Although he was surely the worst judge of his father's appearance — what with him being his son — he couldn't help but believe that they looked nothing alike. His father had blue eyes.

His were brown.

His father had once had light red hair.

Harry had curly blond hair.

"We had you when I was twenty-five, and when your mother was forty-five." He gave a slight smile. "If you think that's shocking these days then you should've seen how it was in the hospital, back then. She always talked about you — about the age difference — about how she feared she would never get to see you growing up." He shook his head. "*Paranoid*, negative, thoughts."

Harry had to restrain the urge to say anything here.

To ask whether his father had any basis to call *someone else* paranoid when he, himself, had decided to hide out here, at The Crosses, for the better portion of his life. Then again, Harry supposed that just about everybody walking the face of the Earth could do with a decent dose of self-awareness.

And he was certainly no exception.

His father's lips parted, as if he was going to add something further.

But he said nothing.

He peered deeply into Harry's eyes for several intense seconds ... and then his gaze drifted beyond, to a side window. Neither of them had thought to close the curtains. No need ... not for reasons of privacy. There were no other houses, not even a public road, in sight.

In the garden.

"Is that ..." his father said.

But Harry was already lifting himself out of his seat.

He was peering out through the glass.

There was someone there.

Someone there.

Suddenly alarmed, he turned back to his father.

"Should I call the police?" his father asked, a panicked look in his eye.

It was one of those looks which Harry knew could only come from a man who spends so much of his time in solitude — away from human companionship. Harry wondered what sorts of fears his father might've built up about the outside world.

"No," Harry replied, and then wondered why he had said it.

He supposed he wanted to show his father he was in control.

That he wasn't about to get carried away.

He had come down from *London*, after all, and if there was anything which distinguished a Londoner from the rest it was that they didn't run away from their problems. They didn't just call the *police*. They dealt with life as it was thrown at them.

Saw what they could do.

And Harry was certain there *was* something he could do.

JOANNE

7.03 PM, SATURDAY

Joanne traced her fingertips across the delicately carved stone statue. It came up to about her waist and featured a cherubic boy — three, four years old. He was naked except for a loincloth which was bunched up about his waist. He stood with his fist clenched firmly, pressed to his hip, looking off in the direction of Goonherth Bay.

It was the expression which was most unsettling about the statue.

How the young boy wore something between a pout and a grimace.

She often wondered if his father was a sailor, and that he was waiting for him to return from sea. To return from some adventure.

The statue had been the centrepiece, too, of course.

The centrepiece for her and Henry's last meeting.

"Hey! Who's there!"

Joanne's heart leaped up to her throat.

Her whole body felt impossibly hot.

And then — all of a sudden — her blood ran cold.

She broke away from the stone statue she had been inspecting, turning in the direction of the cry.

She absorbed the figure, silhouetted by the moonlight shining down on the bay.

She had no need to see his face to know who it was.

Context was enough for her.

She *had* come to *his* house after all ...

"Henry," Joanne began, and then, remembering herself, "... *Harry?*"

Henry stood stock still.

Slowly, Joanne's eyes adjusted to the brightness of the moonlight. She took in what he was wearing. A simple white t-shirt. A pair of jeans. Such garments seemed to be miles away from the image she had built up within her mind.

The image of the City Bigwig.

The man who had a penthouse in Islington.

The man who — it was said — earned millions of pounds a year.

A let-down?

Henry trod toward her. "Is that ... *Joanne?*" He stepped closer still, and then, a dozen or so steps away, he paused, cocked his head to one side. "What're you *doing* here?"

Joanne felt her heart striking her ribs. A tremble caught hold of her whole body. But she managed to keep it from shaking her to the bone. She retained some semblance of control. "I ... heard you were in town."

God, she had never imagined this meeting would be so awkward.

But, then again, just what had she expected?

Had she thought she would get away with simply stalking around in the darkness? Had she *believed* she could just *turn up* at The Crosses and stroll the grounds as if it was her own home?

The ridiculousness of what she was doing only really struck her properly now; now that she had acquiesced to Elena's request ... that she take part in this "plan".

A plan which she didn't even fully understand.

"Are you ... did you ..." Henry said. "I mean" — finally he pressed on a smile — "news spreads fast."

Joanne smiled back. "Goonie isn't a big place."

"Still ... I'm *impressed*."

Unsure what to do with her hands, Joanne began to clasp and unclasp her fingers. She tightened them into fists, feeling her finger-nails digging into her fleshy palms. She glanced about, to where she had allowed her bicycle to collapse on the lawn, beside the statue she had been inspecting. Then she looked back at Henry.

For the first time, she could take in the tightly coiled blond curls; the way he had retained his fresh-faced look despite being in his middle-thirties. People often told Joanne she had retained something of her "girlish" good looks but she was never quite able to see it herself. Whenever she looked in the mirror all she saw were the expression lines about her mouth and eyes. The skin which grew saggier by the day.

Realising that Henry was staring at her intently, surely waiting for her to explain herself, Joanne said, "This place, it ... I don't know ... brings back *memories*, I guess."

" 'Memories' ?" Henry replied, as if he had no idea what she was talking about.

Could he have forgotten so easily?

Joanne *refused* to believe he had forgotten so easily.

But she decided to leave this for now.

She decided it was better for her to stick to the plan.

To do what she'd come here for.

And then leave.

"I suppose you're home for the school reunion?" she asked.

Henry looked deep into her eyes.

Even in the near-darkness she could make out his hazel irises.

How they had a *translucent* quality to them.

Some kind of fantastical *ethereal* quality.

He parted his lips to reply, and then, apparently thinking better of whatever he was about to say, closed them again. He finally answered her question with a curt nod, and a quiet, dry, "That's right."

Joanne looked beyond him, to the moon lingering in the sky, sending its light shimmering across the surface of the Atlantic Ocean beyond. She could feel a light breeze beginning to blow in from the north.

Its chill took her off guard.

She felt almost as if icicles themselves were carried on its torrents.

"Okay," Joanne said, turning back to him, wearing a slight smile. "That's good — that was all I needed to know. All I came here for."

Feeling herself still caught beneath Henry's gaze, she self-consciously went about retrieving her bicycle from where she had allowed it to drop in the grass. The spokes made a *tick-tick* sound as she wheeled it back into an upright position.

She passed Henry, breathing in his clean, male scent.

She thought she could smell some herbs there.

The faintest woody odour of whisky.

She bowed her head and focused on the driveway before her, preparing to mount the bike and freewheel back down to Elena's house — *mission accomplished.*

Joanne had hardly got her leg over the saddle, however, when Henry called her back.

"Jo?" he said.

She had always hated *that* form of her name.

It had always seemed so neutral.

Such a brisk *efficient* way of curtailing what Joanne had always thought was a deeply *feminine* name. But this was hardly the place or time for her to complain ...

She turned back to him.

Realised he was smiling.

She banished the frown which'd seized hold of her lips.

Found it easier than she might've expected to smile back.

"Why didn't you just call?" he asked.

"Oh," she replied, feeling her voice give way for the first time, "I suppose I wanted to see for myself — I suppose I wanted to see *you* for myself."

Henry met her eye for the longest time. As he did so, Joanne couldn't help but feel that he was reading her innermost thoughts.

That he was somehow seeing *exactly* what she was up to.

Finally, Henry let up his intense stare. His gaze softened. "It wouldn't be very gentlemanly of me to turn you away without inviting you in for a drink — now that you've come all this way." He nodded to her bicycle. "No easy undertaking, I know from personal experience."

Joanne hesitated.

She was caught in two minds.

On the one hand, she was conscious of the reason she was here; that her intentions were a long way from honourable. That this *hadn't* been a visit merely for *nostalgia's sake*. But, on the other, she felt an almost magnetic attraction to The Crosses — to Henry himself? — and she felt a nearly irresistible curiosity grip her.

Implore her to take a closer look.

In the end, though, she went with the sensible option. "I need to get back," she said. "My kids ..." This time when she smiled, it wasn't forced. She felt herself blushing too, though she had no real idea why. "I have two girls — they're with their auntie, my sister. She agreed to look after them while I — "

"Did some sleuthing?"

Joanne blushed more deeply still at Henry's response.

Then she gave an innocent shrug.

Henry's smile slipped slightly.

For the first time since he had startled her with his appearance, Joanne felt as if she might be in some sort of danger. As if she might've got herself into a "sticky" situation. She froze up.

Henry broke the tension, though, arching his eyebrow. "Why don't you come in for a drink?" he said. "One for the road?"

Joanne looked off down the driveway, to the elm trees lining it. And then her attention fell on Goonherth Bay just beyond. Back when she'd been a young girl, she'd often played games with that sight. She had told herself that the ocean was like a desert full of quicksand. That, if she so wished, she could launch herself from a nearby cliff, hurl herself into the water, and be sucked down into its endless depths.

Lost forevermore.

She turned back to him.

Smiled.

"Okay, Henry," she said. "Just one."

Henry gestured to the front door. When he set foot on the first step leading up to the door, he halted. Turned to her.

Joanne's heart fluttered at the back of her mouth.

A cold sweat formed on her brow.

She was certain he was going to drop some sort of bombshell.

That he was going to call her out.

Put an end to her game.

Put an end to *Elena's* game.

His expression was so serious.

So *sincere*.

"There's a condition," he said, and then held up a single finger. "*Just one.*"

Joanne held her breath.

Again felt a tremble pass over the surface of her skin.

"What?" she asked.

"It's Harry," he said, with a smirk, treading his way up the steps, turning his back to her. "Call me Harry. I never did like 'Henry', always made me sound like *royalty* ..."

Joanna blinked away her daze.

Caught hold of herself.

She had the presence of mind not to allow her bicycle to tumble free of her hold.

She rested it against the wall of the house and followed him inside.

HENRY
7.14 PM, SATURDAY

I t was a curious situation.

One which Harry never would've thought to anticipate.

Joanne Darkly.

Goodness, it *really had* been a long while. It had been longer than he could even think to get his head around. As he watched her glancing about, taking in the front hall of The Crosses, he couldn't help thinking to himself about how she had hardly changed at all in appearance. She still had that full thick red hair. And those cute, mouselike features. That peachy tone to her complexion. And the sapphire eyes.

The years had indeed been kind to her.

"This way," Harry said, with a slight smile, guiding Joanne along the corridor, in the direction of the drawing room.

As they walked, Harry had to resist the urge to look around at her.

To *take* her in again.

When he had first seen her, out there, in the grounds, he had believed his eyes were playing tricks on him. It had been just like the scene all those years earlier.

An almost *exact* carbon copy.

The *last* time that he had seen Joanne. It had seemed like the beginning of something ... but it had turned out to be the end.

Harry's father rose from the sofa as the two of them strode into the drawing room.

He spread a welcoming smile across his mouth.

A *professional* smile — his father's *performance* smile.

Harry knew that smile so well. He knew how to tell the difference.

There were so many subtle details.

How the smile was wide, and warm, and yet lacking any sort of depth. The smile ended just below his father's cheekbones. It never quite managed to reach his eyes. And yet it seemed that only those closest to him would ever recognise this.

"Ah, I see you've intercepted the trespasser." His father trod closer, still smiling, and then addressed Joanne. "It must've been ten, fifteen years? Longer? How've you been?" He laid a hand on her shoulder before leaning in to plant a kiss on either one of her cheeks.

Joanne flipped Harry a sidelong glance as if to silently ask if his father *really* recalled who she was. Joanne was in for a surprise. One of his father's many talents was his memory. How else might he recall tens of thousands of notes during a concert?

"You were thinking of becoming a lawyer, weren't you? When I saw you last?"

Joanne blinked several times, clearly out of disbelief. "That's right," she said.

"Your mother was Gemma — your father Adam." He closed one eye as if he was some cheap practitioner of parlour tricks.

"That's right," Joanne replied, blushing slightly, and mimicking his smile.

His father paused for a long moment, and then said, "When you were sixteen you had an accident." He furrowed his eyebrows, clearly lost in deep thought. "You have a scar on your inner left thigh."

Harry looked to Joanne.

The blush was fading and she was going slightly pale.

She looked to Harry, and then back to his father.

"... Yes," she said.

Harry slipped his father a glance.

There was no need for words.

The look simply said, *That's enough. Enough for now, Dad.*

Harry's father turned back to Joanne, his hand slipping free of her shoulder where it had rested. He took a step back, inviting her to tread deeper into the room. "Now, onto more important matters. What're you drinking?"

JOANNE

7.20 PM, SATURDAY

There was something eerie — unsettling, even — about the drawing room.

When Joanne had first set foot here, she had felt an odd tingling sensation travel up her spine. Part of that was recollection, of course, some aspect of her memory making it clear that she'd been here before.

That she'd *set foot* in this room before.

Although she was certain that it must be some sort of déjà vu, she couldn't help but believe the drawing room was *precisely* as it had been when she had seen it last.

There were the gilt-framed oil paintings which adorned the walls.

And then there was the regal-red carpet beneath her feet.

The beige furniture with silver trimmings completed her recollection.

It was almost as if she had returned to a museum she had visited decades earlier.

And found that it was exactly the same.

Realising that Henry ... *Harry's* ... father was over at the drinks cabinet, standing prone, waiting for her to make up her mind, she snapped back to reality. "Uh, a gin and tonic would be fine," she said, tagging a polite smile onto the end of her words.

With a nod, Harry's father went about mixing up the drink. She watched him as he poured it out, struck by his delicate, precise — *pianist's* — hands. She was still reeling somewhat from the information which he had dished out about her. Not about her parents, or that she had once had dreams of becoming a lawyer — anybody could've picked up on those. No, it was about the scar she had on her inner left thigh.

Something, she had believed, no one else knew about.

No one except for her husband, her parents, her sister, of course ...

Harry's father handed her the gin and tonic before ushering them all over to an armchair and a sofa across the room. Harry and Joanne took their seats on the sofa while Harry's father sat in the armchair opposite. "Any children?" Harry's father asked.

Joanne nursed her drink. "Two girls," she replied.

"How old?"

"Youngest will be two next month, oldest turned five a couple of months ago."

Harry's father gave a grunt of what Joanne took to be approval, and then shot Harry a knowing glance.

With a sigh, Harry rose to the bait. "Dad's always disappointed when I turn up here without a wife on my arm. And *especially* disappointed he doesn't have any grandchildren to drive him up the wall when I come to visit."

Joanne looked over at Harry's father, seeing that, beyond his easy, pleasant smile, there was something of a murky expression clinging to his eyes. She wondered what it might mean. What Harry's father might be thinking deep down. To be honest, Joanne had always felt something at sea when she turned her attentions to attempting to divine the thoughts of others. Even her own parents were something of a mystery. Although she couldn't precisely put her finger on what it was that bothered Harry's father, she could certainly tell that there *was* something.

Her mind-reading abilities had at least progressed that far.

"What're their names?" Harry's father said, after taking a sip of his whisky.

"Michelle and Tabitha — *Tabby*."

Again, Harry's father gave a slight grumble of approval.

After the short exchange, the three of them slipped into silence. Joanne supposed it was because they had nothing in common. The only thing which tied her and Harry together was the fact that they'd attended the same school. Nothing else. Harry had left to go and make his fortune while Joanne had stayed here.

In Goonherth Bay.

Joanne judged that it was about a minute's worth of silence before Harry's father got up from his place in the armchair, crossed the room, and, with a yawn, deposited his empty glass on the counter of the drinks cabinet. "If you'll excuse me," he said, "I think I'll head up to bed." He gave a slight smile, and then ventured out the room.

As he did so, Joanne couldn't help noticing what he was wearing.

Strange that it hadn't registered with her before.

Harry's father wore a dressing gown over the top of a white shirt, and black dress trousers. She couldn't help but think that he looked as if he was preparing for a concert; as if he was ready — at a moment's notice — to give a recital.

Before she could reflect any further, he was gone, and the sound of crumpling paper distracted her. She turned her head to look and saw that Harry had produced a scrunched-up letter from his pocket. She recognised it instantly when he unfolded it. She saw that it was the official invitation from Saint Camelgal *High School*.

The school which she and Harry had attended.

It had been months since she had seen the letter.

She had sent off the reply slip expressing her wish to attend the twenty-year reunion. It had seemed like a bit of fun. A chance for her to reflect on how everyone else had got on with their lives. What sorts of messes they had got themselves into.

"This must be the reunion you were talking about," Harry said.

Joanne was confused for a couple of moments. She thought that Harry had somehow drifted off into another realm. When she had asked him the reason why he'd come home, he'd told her that it'd been for the reunion. Or had she just put words in his mouth? Had she only provided him with a convenient alibi?

Harry laid the letter flat on the sofa cushion between them.

The reply slip was still very much intact.

Harry hadn't confirmed his attendance.

With a sigh, he explained, "My father only handed me the letter earlier today." He shrugged. "I guess the school still believes I'm staying in my bedroom in my parents' house." He fired a glance at Joanne — almost a look of accusation. "Makes you wonder whether anybody who went to our school succeeded in life, doesn't it?"

Not thinking quickly enough to respond in any satisfactory way, Joanne could only nod in agreement. She *did* have her own house, thankfully, although it *was* heavily mortgaged. It was true to say, though, that her letter had arrived at her parents' house.

There was a long, drawn-out silence, and Joanne decided there was no reason for her not to break it. "If you didn't come home for the class reunion then why did you come home?"

Harry stared into his near empty glass, the last trickle of tangerine nectar — whisky — glistening in the bottom. He drew a deep breath. Then sighed it out. "Oh," he replied, "my mother's dying."

Joanne's gut sank. She regretted asking the question now. "I'm sorry."

"Hmm."

"Is there, you know, anything ... what ... I mean ..."

But there was nothing for Joanne to say.

Thankfully Harry picked up the slack. "I got here about lunchtime, you know? I went up to see her soon as I arrived — "

On instinct, Joanne rose. "Oh, you mean she's here? In the *house?*"

Harry met her eye. Nodded dolefully. "Upstairs, in her room."

"I should ... it's getting late ..."

Harry said nothing in reply. He only patted the sofa, beckoning her to sit again. "What's the rush?" he asked. "It's early yet." He paused, met her eye for the briefest of moments, and then asked, "Is your husband waiting for you?"

"No."

"Your boyfriend?"

"No."

"*Girl*friend?"

"No!" Joanne shot back, unable to prevent a giggle sneaking out. "Shut up!"

She felt a strange tingle run through her veins.

One of those *adolescent* kicks.

Like those which would accompany first kisses.

Intimate caresses.

"Then," Harry said, "what's the rush?"

Joanne wanted to say something about her two girls. She had promised her sister who was babysitting that she would be back before ten.

When she glanced across the room, noted the large grandfather clock propped up against the wall, she saw she still had *plenty* of time.

Plenty of time for *what?*

As the two of them recovered from the "high spirits", or whatever it had been which'd passed between them, Harry continued where he'd left off. "After going to see her, I came down here with Dad. We talked all afternoon." He nodded to the drinks cabinet. "That bottle of whisky was near enough full when I arrived."

Joanne noted only about a quarter of the bottle remained.

It was a wonder Harry and his father were able to speak, let alone stand.

"I haven't even been up to my bedroom yet," Harry continued. "Haven't even had a chance to lug my bag up there."

Joanne's shoulders went stiff.

Her whole body felt unmoveable.

But she met Harry's gaze all the same.

"Will you come up with me?" he asked, then smiled. "I need someone to hold my hand." He peered back down into his glass. "You know, just in case there's a ghost, or a monster, or something?"

ELENA

7.36 PM, SATURDAY

Standing in her mother's kitchen, Elena felt herself trembling all over. She could hardly believe what was happening. What it was that they were all planning.

But she wasn't in two minds.

She was certain that this was the way that things needed to be done.

This was her chance. A chance for her, Max and Jock to get back at Henry Foldes.

To show him that they *mattered*.

That he wasn't the untouchable figure he believed himself to be.

The cups of tea clinked together as she carried them through the corridor to the sitting room. Upstairs she could already hear her mother snoring. No doubt she had lain down in the bed alongside George's cot and simply drifted off to sleep.

That made Elena feel better.

She felt *much* better to know that her mother wouldn't overhear what she and the two men were about to discuss. Some things needed to remain a secret from parents.

Forever, if possible.

She handed over the tea.

Jock took his black, no milk, no sugar, while Max had requested five spoons of sugar and a splash of cream. Since Elena wasn't in the habit of judging, she had acquiesced to his request.

They all sat around in the sitting room, sipping on their tea.

It was Jock who eventually spoke up.

Elena had noticed that he had a tick, that while he was thinking of something to say, he would absentmindedly twirl his ponytail around his finger. He was doing this now. "I'm glad you asked us here," he said. "I mean, I'm glad that we have this *opportunity*."

Max said nothing, occupying himself with chugging down the entire contents of his tea in one go.

From their conversation so far, Elena had learned that Max and Jock had both left Goonherth Bay behind long ago, and that they were successful in their own ways. That Max was a regional manager of some carpentry enterprise while Jock had gone far as a computer programmer. She had averted questions about their private lives, worried she might be overstepping her remit. They were all here on businesslike terms, after all.

Wasn't revenge always that way?

"I'm not gonna lie," Jock said, "it's taken me many years of therapy to get past ... *things*."

This statement brought silence to bear on the room.

Elena felt her chest tighten.

A chill ran through her bloodstream.

On instinct, not because she consciously thought it the direction the conversation needed to head, she turned to Max. As if prompted, he nodded at her. His eyes were watery. There was no reason for him to say anything further. It was obvious he was affected — that he had been *afflicted* in the same manner as Jock.

Elena? She had only been a witness.

But a necessary one ...

"We could've said something," Elena put in. "Could've gone to the police."

But her words died almost as soon as they had tumbled free of her lips.

Who would've believed them?

Just an accident ... that was all it had been.

A pair of *unfortunate* accidents.

They had all almost finished their tea when Jock finally spoke up.

"I guess I was always aware that Henry was a bully — that he was *my* bully ... and yet ... I don't know ... it never seemed to be anything that needed dealing with." Jock glanced up. "Do you understand what I'm saying?"

Elena couldn't say she did, but she noticed Max bow his head in agreement.

Jock went on, as if this had turned into some sort of peer-support group. "I worked out ways to cope with what was going on." He blinked rapidly as if he was seeing himself in some past form — in his *teenage* form. "Every morning, I remember so clearly, I would look at myself in the mirror, and I would say to myself, out loud, *Don't let him push you around — don't let anyone push you around.*" He shook his head. "Of course I'd always allow him to push me around all the same ... but it seemed that it was important for me to say the words. Otherwise it would all remain bottled up. Otherwise I might not find the will, you know, the will to *go on.*"

Again, Elena shifted a glance to Max.

Saw that his head was still bowed.

Jock continued, "I can still remember the first day that Henry picked on me. So clearly." He gave a smile — a wry smirk. "It was PE. Rugby. Year Eight. September. About this time of year. It was colder then, though. There was frost on the ground. I was still young enough — *naive enough* — to not really mind rolling about on frozen ground, chasing a misshapen ball. I remember it was before any of the boys had grown significantly bigger than others. We were all on a level playing field to some extent, or a more level playing field than in later years."

He flared his nostrils and stared at an undefined spot on the carpet as if he was seeing the images in his mind's eye flicker before him like a projector.

"When Henry hit me with that tackle, he knocked the air right out of me. Even when I was tumbling through the air, his arms about my waist, all his force plunging me down, I was still smiling ... still holding the ball tight to my chest. I could remember thinking that I was having a good time. That I was *enjoying* the game. But it was when I lay on the floor, still holding onto the ball, with the throbbing pain in my left shoulder that I caught a look at Henry's face as he stood over me." He shook his head. "Hatred — *pure* hatred. There are no other words to describe it."

In the house, Elena thought she heard something stirring.

George turning over in his sleep.

Perhaps her mother speaking while she dreamed. She did that sometimes.

Neither Jock or Max seemed to have heard the sound.

"I knew it was the beginning of something — that I had done *something* to draw Henry's attention." Jock shrugged. "Maybe it's because I've always been a lanky streak of piss, that could have some-thing to do with it. Or maybe I was just some random target." He smirked. "Convenient prey."

Elena glanced to Max, expecting him to contribute something to this conversation.

Speak about his own experiences with Henry as his bully.

But he remained still.

Unnaturally still.

Finally, he spoke up, his voice so quiet that Elena almost asked him to raise his tone. But she could just about make out what he said.

"What do you have planned?" Max asked. "What do you want to *do* to him?"

Elena breathed in. She allowed her chest to inflate.

To draw in the heaviness hanging over the room.

"I thought I would leave that to you two," she replied. "He was your bully, after all."

HENRY

8.02 PM, SATURDAY

Harry had only been half joking about wanting someone to hold his hand on his way up to his bedroom.

Back when he was a child, he had been close to terrified of the prospect of mounting the creaking spiral stairs and going up to his room on the second storey of the west wing. What he hadn't revealed to anybody was how the fear had never really left him. How still to this day he held something of a fear about being alone here.

About coming up here alone.

Especially at night.

On his way, he flipped on lights.

He breathed in the stilted air.

He felt the gentle weight of the suitcase he had brought up with him from the front hall. It felt good for him to have a large blunt object so close. It gave him a sense of safety. Of *security*.

Each time he felt his stomach sinking, he turned back and looked to Joanne. Was it just him or had she grown more beautiful with the years? It was hard for him to believe her — that she didn't have a boyfriend or a husband, nothing like that.

Who would leave such a glorious piece of feminine beauty to the sharks?

There he went again ... Harry couldn't help but think that some of the City attitudes were rubbing off on him. When he had first arrived in the City he had known all about the sleazy goings-on and he had attempted to distance himself from such things. And, in truth, he only ever indulged in vices — girls, drugs, booze — whenever the client made it a necessity.

He had thought that he'd put those things behind him.

He'd thought that he'd *fixed* those things ...

Hadn't that been one of the points of going away; of putting distance between himself and his past?

When they stood outside his bedroom door, Harry paused.

He wasn't certain what to do next.

If he should try and kiss Joanne.

How would she take such an action?

Surely the fact that she had come over here, of her own volition, demonstrated that she was interested ... that she was practically *throwing* herself at him.

And yet, he couldn't quite bring himself to do such a thing.

It seemed almost as if he was treading on the toes of his teenage self.

Of his teenage *commitments*.

He still recalled *that* particular day.

Since his birthday was toward the end of July, it had happily coincided with the end of the exams, and thus the end of school. It had been no real challenge to convince his parents to allow him to have a party both to celebrate the end of school and his sixteenth birthday. What he hadn't quite been able to believe was the way in which his father had thrown himself into the proceedings. How he had put all his creative powers to the task of preparing a perfect celebration for his only son.

His only child.

It had always been set up as a bookend.

As the End of an Era.

And so it had proven to be.

Now that he was here, with Joanne, it felt almost like he was finishing what he had failed to do so many years earlier.

When he turned the doorknob, and led her into his bedroom, instead of looking over the decor he knew so well — the decor which he knew would've been unmoved since the last time he'd been here — he studied Joanne.

To begin with she struck a neutral expression.

She gave nothing away.

Her eyes gently twitched about their sockets.

Slowly taking it all *in*.

The bed, lying close to the bare floorboards.

The sloping roof above their heads.

And the window which occupied a large portion of the room.

The one which looked out over the garden.

And Goonherth Bay.

All things considered, Harry supposed this would be the bedroom of most teenage boys' dreams. It was far flung, distant from his parents' portion of the house. He had his own bathroom nearby. He even had his own set of stairs. If either of his parents had ever approached his bedroom he would hear them long before they arrived ... the creaking steps would see to that.

Actually, he supposed it would be the bedroom of most people's dreams.

He was watchful of Joanne as she trod the floorboards, making them creak slightly as she drank in more and more of the details. They had been alone here.

Twenty years ago.

But they had been interrupted.

Now was their chance ... a chance for them to be alone *again*.

Harry laid the suitcase down at his feet. He had everything he needed nestled within it. He could easily see out a week, or longer, if he was required here.

When he turned to Joanne, he saw she was taking in the view over the bay. All the girls he'd ever brought up to his bedroom had been captivated by *that* sight. They had all wanted to watch the sunrise reflected on the bay; as the sun rose behind the house.

In reality, though, they would almost never be capable of staying up late enough.

They would simply be too *exhausted*.

It made him smile to think of those days.

He had been so *young* then.

So *energetic*.

Those nights Harry had always stayed up to watch the sunrays dancing over the bay. He had always found the strength to lie awake. In truth, he had never trusted anyone enough to allow himself to fall asleep in their presence ... to be *exposed* in their company. He had never been able to get over the irrational fear that his lover might slip a knife in between his ribs.

Irrational ... but very real.

Perhaps it was time that he return to therapy.

Maybe he had found someone it would be worth returning to therapy *for*.

At first, he thought it was the whisky speaking. But, in the end, he decided he still possessed something within him.

Something sincere.

Something which *wouldn't* be killed.

"Joanne Darkly," he said. "The one who got away."

He hadn't bothered to flip on the lights, not wanting to spoil the view out of the window. But even in the relative darkness, he could tell that Joanne was blushing. He moved closer and was surprised when she backed away. As if there was something about him which repelled. Which meant that he couldn't come any closer.

Harry knew when it was better to play it slowly — to be *calm*.

Now was one of those moments.

Finally, she turned to him.

Met his eyes.

"Are you coming to the school reunion?" Joanne asked.

Harry felt himself taken aback, both by the directness of the question, and how she seemed somehow *intense* in her manner ... as if she was ready to *bleed* the answer from him. "I already said I was ..."

"Mm," she replied, staring right back.

He knew he couldn't bullshit her so easily so he reassessed his approach.

What time?" he asked.

"Midday. It finishes at four."

Harry felt his stomach dip.

He recalled just why he was here.

Why he was really here.

"It depends," he replied. "Depends how Mum's doing ... I need to be here for her."

"Tell me you'll go."

Again, Harry was taken off guard by the intensity of her tone of voice.

He wondered what the subtext might be.

What he might be promising himself to ... and then he lost himself in her eyes.

Everything else just seemed to *melt* away.

"I'll go," he finally replied.

Joanne launched herself forward, planting her lips against his own.

Harry was unnerved by such sudden passion and wasn't sure how to manage it.

And then he reminded himself to kiss her back — to be as strong as she was.

He would not allow anyone to dominate him.

Not even Joanne Darkly.

MAX

8.24 PM, SATURDAY

Max Yardsman listened to Elena and Jock continue to speak among themselves in the sitting room. He trod carefully along the corridor, soon tracking down the toilet.

It was a tight room, with a window looking out onto the darkened garden.

He shut the door behind him.

Began to feel alone again.

Began to feel *normal* again.

Although he couldn't have arrived more than three hours ago, it seemed as if a lifetime had passed since he had arrived here.

A nearly unstoppable urge plagued him now, demanding that he go.

That he leave this place.

That he get himself as far away from Goonherth Bay as was possible ...

Just what on Earth had possessed him to believe that it would be a good idea to return for the school reunion?

Had he indeed held some subconscious longing — a desire which he dared not speak aloud — which drew him back to Henry Foldes.

As if the two were *linked* in some way?

With infinite care, Max reached into his jacket.

From the inside pocket, he withdrew the flick knife he had purchased from a service station on the drive here. It had been an impulse buy — well before Elena had got into contact with him. Well before she had asked him over to discuss "revenge".

He stared at himself in the mirror, holding the flick knife up beside his face.

Still staring himself in the eye, he jabbed the release button.

The blade flicked free.

He gazed at it.

Polished.

The edge sharp.

He imagined the knife was designed for camping; that the majority of people passing through the service station would be holidaymakers. They wouldn't be returning home with the foggy notion of settling a life-long grudge.

For a moment, Max was hypnotised.

He held the knife up to one eye and peered along the edge.

A voice, somewhere at the back of his mind, implored him to test its sharpness.

Another voice — the voice of *reason* — brought him back.

Spoke *sense* to him.

Max was glad for that voice ... without it, he was certain he would've ceased to be years ago. Without that voice of reason yesterday afternoon, when he had lost his job, he might've gone and done something rash. He might've *lost his mind* ...

But he had held it together.

Managed to keep his feet on the ground.

Or so it seemed.

As if he was handling something impossibly delicate, Max gently closed the flick knife. He replaced it in the inside pocket of his jacket.

For later.

Just in *case*.

Finally, he turned his attention to the job at hand. He wondered how anxious others got about something so simple as visiting a toilet.

About *taking a leak ...*

With the same level of care he'd taken with the flick knife, Max unbuttoned his trousers and eased the fly open. He took in the specially adapted underwear with a zipper down the front. He gently eased the zipper open.

Although it was a sight which Max was greeted by many times in the course of the day, he still felt waves of aftershock jangle his nerves. To find himself staring at the reminder of what Henry Foldes had done to him.

How Henry Foldes had *afflicted* his life.

The deformed, half-destroyed penis.

The single remaining testicle.

Melted skin.

A shudder danced down his spine.

He cursed Henry Foldes, just as he did every day. He thought back to *that* chemistry lesson. How Henry Foldes, in the company of those faceless cronies — all of those *boys* who'd egged him on — had hurled the beaker of acid at Max's crotch.

Just to bring the memory to mind sent a shiver through Max's whole body.

Even though his physical therapist had told him it was just his imagination, he was certain that he still had sensation in his groin. That he could *still* feel the hot, burning pain which'd been brought on by the acid.

At school, the whole matter had been referred to as an "incident"
...

And then an *accident.*

It had only been Henry and his cronies in the classroom at the time.

The only witnesses.

And like the cronies they were they had defended him.

Made it seem as though Max had done this to himself.

Max recalled how he was treated throughout the investigation process.

How when he brought up the possibility that this had been a purposeful attack, one of the "experts" involved had told him that "memory manipulation" was a common side-effect of such an "unfortunate accident".

But Max *knew* what he had seen.

It still stretched his mind to think about Jock.

About how Henry had not only been allowed to get away with what he had done to him, but how he had been allowed to repeat the process.

To mutilate another boy's genitals.

Mostly Max just felt anger.

At Henry, at the school ... and at *everything* and *everyone* which surrounded it.

Max gritted his teeth, allowed his eyes to narrow to slits.

He worked the muscles.

He willed the urine out of him — *drop by drop*.

Listened to the unsatisfactory, staccato splashes in the toilet bowl. When he felt he had relieved himself sufficiently, he gently dabbed at his afflicted manhood with a wad of toilet paper and went back through the same process as before.

The process of *zipping himself up* ...

When he caught his own eye in the mirror, he felt humiliated.

Even though he was *alone*.

And wasn't some anonymous fat kid any longer.

He had grown into an adult.

One with thoughts, and feelings, and opinions.

And dreams.

... And *dreams*.

What right did memories have to affect his life?

When Max left to re-join Elena and Jock, he realised he didn't feel angry.

No, he felt a much *cooler* emotion than that.

All he felt was a vague ... *void* ... as if he had done all of the feeling he could muster.

At least in this life.

Now there came ... something else ...

Just what that "something" might be, Max couldn't say.

Not yet, anyway.

ELENA

11.36 PM, SATURDAY

It had been a good couple of hours since Elena had waved Jock and Max off from her doorstep. She had observed them take off in opposite directions. Both of them had seemed somewhat dejected once they had left her behind, although that was understandable. They *were* talking about Henry Foldes, here ...

To tell the truth, Elena wasn't too concerned about Jock or Max, she was more worried about what'd become of Joanne. She hadn't seen her since she had seen her off five, six hours ago. Joanne hadn't taken her phone with her, mumbling something to Elena about how she wanted to "show trust" ... just how Joanne would show "trust" by not taking her phone along with her genuinely escaped Elena. In the past half hour alone, Joanne's mobile had rung seven or eight times. Although Elena hadn't intruded so far as to answer the call, she had seen it was Beth — Joanne's sister — who had been ringing.

Just as Elena felt a yawn beginning to take hold of her mouth, she realised she could hear a sound off in the street. That was the thing about Goonherth Bay, one of those things which Elena had forgotten when she had ventured into bigger cities, that an almost oppressive silence hung over the place after dark.

Everyone tucked up in bed by nine.

Elena shifted through the house, checking in again on the guest room. She saw her mother and George continued to sleep away, as they had throughout the evening. She descended the stairs, catching a whiff of the delicious food which her mother had been cooking up earlier that day, and wondering if she should serve herself just a *little* more.

When Elena reached the sitting room, she looked out through the curtains.

To the street outside.

She soon made out the advancing figure.

The bicycle she wheeled along at her side.

Joanne.

Elena felt a rush of mixed emotions as she jogged to the door, as she undid the latch and waited for Joanne. When Joanne was near enough for the two of them to speak without shouting, Elena let out a stifled, "What *happened?*"

Joanne said nothing right away, continuing to trail her bike alongside her. "Puncture," she said, as if this explained everything. "Had to walk."

Indeed, when Elena did look to the bike, she saw one of the tyres had gone flat.

Joanne left the bike up against the side of the house and then trod in past Elena.

As Joanne brushed by, Elena couldn't help but note that sickly sweet scent clinging to her.

Sex.

The *smell* of sex.

"Anyone call?" Joanne asked, mostly to herself as she flipped a quick glance over her shoulder while picking up her phone.

"Just your sister."

Joanne parted her lips in an "oh" shape, taking in the screen. She brought her hand up to her forehead, as if administering a cold compress. "Jesus, is that the time?"

Elena said nothing.

She remained standing there.

"What happened?" Elena asked.

Joanne, however, was already tapping away at her phone, occupied.

Elena waited out the time patiently. "Is he coming to the reunion tomorrow?"

Joanne looked up briefly. "Maybe."

" '*Maybe*' ?" Elena replied, with a glare, and taking a couple of steps closer.

Joanne said nothing else, busily tapping out a message — apparently to her sister.

In the near silence, broken only by the sound of calloused fingertips against mobile phone screen, Elena decided to stop being so coy. She decided to cut through the fog. "You didn't ... did you?"

Joanne looked away from the screen now, her attention suddenly fully focused on Elena. "What's it to you?" she said, a touch of bile to her tone.

Impulsively, Elena recoiled from Joanne.

She knew *that* tone well, of course.

She recognised it from their school days.

Although Elena never would've stretched herself to say that Joanne had been a bully, she had certainly never treated her with anything but loathing and derision. Had the mere act of Joanne going to see Henry Foldes brought all of this back?

Had what she had *done* with Henry Foldes brought the past back to life?

Joanne finished up her message, and, apparently realising her mistake — that she had been a little quick with her tone — she turned to Elena with a more familiar smile. "Listen," she said, "it was nothing. It was ... I don't know ... it just felt as if it was the *end* of something. The end of something which was a long time coming."

Elena resisted the urge to reply.

Joanne's phone buzzed. She checked it quickly, arched an

eyebrow. "Shit," she said, "seems like my sis is seriously pissed." She glanced back up at Elena. "Guess I'd better get shoving off — don't want to find that she's gone postal, or whatever, I've grown quite attached to those kids of mine."

Elena wasn't really in the mood for Joanne's "special" brand of sarcasm.

She didn't currently have the mental resources to deal with *colours* of meaning.

She wanted to see things as they were.

In black and white.

As Joanne made her way along the hallway, back to her afflicted bicycle, leaning up against the outside wall, Elena reached out on impulse and took hold of the sleeve of Joanne's blouse.

Joanne flinched, as if Elena had hit her with all the force of a punch.

"Did he hurt you?" Elena asked, keeping her voice as plain, as *reasonable*, as she could manage.

Joanne met her eyes. " 'Hurt me' ?" She widened her eyes. "What'd you mean?"

Elena said nothing. She had already said enough.

Perhaps she had said *too much*.

Nobody spoke about what'd happened.

Nobody spoke about what *Henry Foldes* had done to them.

Joanne glanced down at where Elena held the sleeve of her blouse. She gave a slight smile. "You reckon you could, you know, let go of me?"

Elena held on tightly. Continued to meet Joanne's eyes.

"You're not ... *jealous*, are you, El?"

Finally, Elena found her voice. "Jealous? No, why would I be *jealous*?"

Joanne said nothing. She averted Elena's gaze. Shook her head. "I don't know, it's weird — you know — to drag all of this school stuff back up again. It does strange things with the mind." She met Elena's eye again. "At least I can say it's been doing weird things to *my* mind."

"I just want to know if he did anything to you — anything *violent*."

Joanne's eyes glassed over.

Elena felt the strength in her grip give way.

Joanne slipped away from her, continued on out of the door. She only turned back to speak with Elena when she was halfway down the garden path, wheeling her bicycle alongside. "You should get some sleep, El. Get some rest. You look like you need it." And then, with a frail smile, Joanne walked off past the front gate, and into the street.

Elena continued to stare off at Joanne until she had disappeared from view.

Then she turned around and went back inside.

HENRY

12.14 AM, SUNDAY

Harry struggled to keep himself still — to stop himself from trembling.

This had to have been one of the most overwhelming days of his life.

When he had woken up this morning, found that message from his father, he never would've expected to end the day in the arms of Joanne Darkly.

Joanne.

Darkly.

Harry plodded along the corridor, headed for his parents' bedroom.

He felt strangely at peace with himself.

After he had walked Joanne to the door, offered her a ride home by car — and after she had refused him — he had returned to the drawing room, had another few sips of whisky. A night cap. He had needed to fire up some courage for what was to come.

For *this* moment now.

He stood for the longest time outside the door. Although it was true to say that he had never felt completely comfortable at The

Crosses — that it had never been his "home" — he had never before felt as alien, as out of place, as he did now.

He didn't *fit* here, that much was certain.

"Harry?"

A skitter ran up his spine. He turned to look.

Saw his father standing in the darkness.

He had appeared seemingly out of nowhere.

Apparently seeing his confusion, his father explained himself. "I've been sleeping in one of the guest rooms," he said. "Your mother needs her space. And I ... well, I suppose I need *my* space too — a chance for me to rest."

Harry said nothing.

His father wore the same dressing gown he had had on previously, only this time he wore pyjamas beneath instead of the white shirt and formal black trousers. From the dark bags which clung to the bottoms of his father's eyes, he wondered if his father had slept at all, or if he had simply been staring up at the ceiling through the darkness.

"Can I go in and see her?" Harry asked.

"Of course you can. Don't know if she's awake, though."

Feeling his father's gaze laying heavily over him, Harry turned the doorknob and stepped inside. He left the door open and his father followed him in.

Harry stood at the foot of the bed, looking at his mother, watching as she lay on her back, breathing heavily, bundled up in blankets.

He wished he could do something.

He wished there *was* something for him to do.

He glanced to his father, and then, noting the direction of his father's gaze, he turned his attention onto the metal tray which lay on the bedside table.

All of those syringes.

Glass vials.

Painkillers.

"I just wanted to say goodnight." His throat dried up. "I wanted to *kiss* her goodnight."

His father replied only with a nod.

Harry rounded the bed, leaned down to his mother. He planted a kiss on her forehead, feeling the wrinkled, leathery quality of her skin against his lips.

His heart beat against the underside of his throat.

Blood rushed to his temples.

It became a struggle to draw air into his lungs.

He straightened up.

When he looked to his father, he saw he was focused on Harry's mother.

Harry realised her eyes were open.

That she was looking at *him*.

His mother brought her trembling hands free of the blankets.

He was relegated to the status of observer as her pallid, birdlike hand reached for him. Reached for his cheeks.

Her fingers were cold.

They chilled his blood.

From between withered lips, he heard her voice.

"Son. My *son*."

It was as if someone had jabbed a needle directly into Harry's heart.

To hear her voice ... to hear her voice *again*.

He had believed he never would ...

Her eyelids drooped.

Her strength would soon desert her.

And her consciousness would slip.

He made out the final words she murmured before slipping away into sleep again.

"You ... *came back*."

Harry felt a fizzling sensation in his gut.

Something about her words carried a note of finality.

As if he had accomplished some great feat.

As if he had completed an epic journey.

It had only been a five-hour drive.

He could be back in London in time for breakfast if he wanted ...

He gave his now-sleeping mother a parting kiss and retreated from the room.

ELENA

E lena awoke with a start.

Her son George's eyes stared into hers.

Big and blue.

He smiled wide.

For several seconds, Elena was confused about how George had managed to get here. How he had come to lie on her stomach. He wasn't able to crawl yet.

She had believed he'd been upstairs, sleeping.

The scene finally cleared and she absorbed the periphery.

Noted that her mother stood there.

That she was holding him on her chest.

Elena had fallen asleep on the sofa, in the sitting room.

"Good morning," her mother said, in Hungarian.

Elena greeted her in English.

George gave a babble of glee as Elena's mother hoisted him up from her stomach.

Elena eyed them as they crossed the sitting room and disappeared through the doorway into the kitchen. Her mother said something about breakfast being ready.

76

Elena felt sick to the stomach.

She must have simply collapsed on the sofa after Joanne had left; fallen into an uneasy sleep. The morning sunlight streamed over her face.

When she finally rose, of course still wearing the same clothes she'd had on the day before, she took in the blazing blue skies stretching across Goonherth Bay and knew the warm weather was set to continue. That it would, most likely, turn out to be a perfect day for the school reunion.

Was she even sure she wanted to go?

With that thought fixed on her mind, she shifted in the general direction of the bathroom — *upstairs* — fending off her mother's demands that she "eat something".

In the bathroom, Elena undressed, depositing her worn, slept-in clothes on the tiled floor. She stepped into the shower cubicle and turned the water on full.

Instantly, a high-pressured jet of pleasantly warm water poured down on her.

She soaked her head and hair, bringing her face up into the constant flow.

It was a kind of aquatic massage.

Relaxing after the sleep-deprived night she had suffered.

As always, her towel hung off the warming rail in the bathroom. She stepped out of the shower and reached for it, bringing it about her waist and chest. She wrapped herself up warm, beginning the process of getting dry.

Once she had dried the upper half of her body, she switched her focus to the lower. She started at her feet, taking care to get the spaces between her toes as dry as she could manage. And then she shifted her attention to her legs.

Worked her way upwards, slowly.

It was when she reached her left inner thigh that she paused.

That she had to suck in some air.

It was almost as if the wound was fresh.

Almost as if ... as if she had just woken up in Henry Foldes's bed.

And found the sheets damp with blood.

Her blood.

When she thought of the gash she had located on her thigh, the blood seeping from the wound, a fresh giddiness struck her. But she managed to stay on her feet.

She wasn't going to go full Renaissance Woman all of a sudden ... not now.

She needed to keep it together.

Even if it was just for one day.

She blinked away the memories, gently draping the towel over the long-ago healed scar on her thigh. Although it no longer hurt — it *had* been twenty years, after all — she still felt a twinging sensation at the back of her mind only to look at the scar.

She didn't even need to physically *touch* it ...

She thought about what'd happened later on that day.

How the house had been deserted.

How The Crosses had been deserted.

No sign of Henry Foldes, or his family.

Elena had located some cotton wool in a nearby bathroom and she had created herself a makeshift dressing. She had pressed the soft material to the bleeding wound.

And then she had limped through the house.

Limped her way down the drive.

Gone to the doctor's office.

Had the wound cleaned, stitches put in.

She had only told one person the full story.

Her mother.

When she had told her mother what had transpired, her reaction was just as Elena would've imagined. Just as she had *feared* it might be.

Her mother, like any responsible, loving parent, had wanted her to go to the police, to tell them what had happened. What Henry Foldes had done to her.

But Elena hadn't wanted to cause a fuss.

Well, that was how she had explained it to herself.

In reality, she had *feared* Henry Foldes.

She *still* feared Henry Foldes.

That was why she had called Max, Jock and Joanne together last night.

She was afraid to face him alone.

Elena put the thoughts out of her mind and turned her attention back to the matter at hand. What was to come later on today.

The school reunion.

She would see everyone again.

She would see *him* again.

Was she ready?

There was still time to back out ...

JOCK

9.40 AM, SUNDAY

Jock Jones laid out the two suits he had brought with him for the purposes of the school reunion. He had laid out one suit on each of the twin beds in the bed and breakfast he'd spent the night in. Although his parents lived just around the corner, he had decided that he preferred to stay apart from them.

He liked to have his space.

Space for his *computers*; the two of them stood over on the desk, both running through various programs. Working for him even on a Saturday morning.

He had woken early this morning — around six — and made the bed he had slept in. It proved impossible to break free of his weekday routine even on the weekend ... he could tell his body was anticipating his daily trip to the gym. It was anticipating him wanting to work up a sweat, and then to take a cold shower before slipping into his work clothes. That was how he got prepared for the day.

But the bed and breakfast had no gym.

And neither did Goonherth Bay.

Not one which was open to the public, in any case.

He had toyed with the idea of forgetting the invitation had even appeared in his post one day. He had wondered if he chose to simply bury his head in the sand, to ignore the invitation completely, that it would somehow disappear.

In fact, there had been one notable moment when he had crunched the invitation — envelope and all — into a tight ball and thrown it into a bin in his office at work. It hadn't been until later on in the day that he had had second thoughts and he had had to go and embarrassingly plead with the cleaners to allow him to paw through the plastic sacks of rubbish they had gathered earlier in the day. He had found the invitation, the reply slip still stapled to the letter.

Later that day he had replied in the affirmative.

That he *would* attend the reunion.

And he had regretted it ever since.

Why he had beaten himself up so badly about accepting the invitation to the school reunion escaped him somewhat. After all, he was his own master. He had no girlfriend, no wife, no *family* of his own.

Only his parents, left back here, in Goonherth Bay.

There was nobody *compelling* him to return home for the school reunion ... and yet, at the same time, there was a part of him — some nagging voice — which refused to give him peace. Some part of him which would see it as a great failure if he didn't attend the school reunion. If he didn't face up to his past.

If he didn't face up to his enemies.

And so here he was ...

No backing out now.

He would never forgive himself if he *did* back out.

Even though there was nobody sharing the room with him, and the curtains were drawn closed, Jock wore his undervest and Y-front underwear. He had always had a thing about *being naked* ... especially when he was away from his flat.

He felt exposed.

As if someone could knock on the door at any moment.

Call out to him.

There was a disquieting feature of the room, too, in the form of the full-length mirror which hung from one of the walls. Jock had done his best to avoid mirrors whenever he could. In his flat, he had only a modest-sized bathroom mirror, one which only showed off his upper torso. Nothing more.

He never needed to *see* any more.

Now, though, today of all days, it felt as if it might be the right time.

As if he shouldn't put this off any longer.

Just who was he trying to fool?

Because he certainly couldn't fool himself ...

Decided, Jock gently slipped down his underwear. He stared himself in the eye as he did so, unsure what he was afraid of. What he had been afraid of all these years.

It was *his* body, after all.

When he had slipped his underwear all the way down to his ankles, he shook it off, allowing it to drop onto the floor. To be collected later.

He stood naked before the mirror.

Seeing himself.

His *image* staring back at him.

Slowly, his eyes moved downward.

He breathed in profoundly.

Allowed himself a moment to clear his thoughts.

And then he looked.

He made out the scarring on the underside of his penis. It was distinctive, and not easily missed. The scar aside, though, his penis was unharmed.

The real damage had been done further below.

Jock shut his eyes so tightly he could barely see out through the slits. He observed the odd, fleshy mass which hung beneath his penis.

Not quite testicles.

As he took in the sight, he felt tears beginning to seep out of the corners of his eyes. A single one broke free and streaked his cheek.

He could still see that day.

He still *dreamed* about that day.

It had been a PE lesson.

Just another class.

One of those never-ending days in the middle of summer.

There had been nothing remarkable about the class itself. Only that Jock had been especially tired after having run the 1600m. The same could've been said for any of his classmates. He had been running behind getting changed because he'd picked up a slight knock. As he had turned one of the bends during the run, he had felt something in his ankle give.

A tendon?

Some muscle?

He had no idea, but the upshot of the matter had been that he'd been diverted to the nurse's office. Once he'd got the all-clear, after demonstrating he still had a full range of motion with the joint, and no *extreme* pain, he had returned to the changing rooms.

Jock recalled very clearly what he'd been thinking about.

He couldn't wait until he got home.

Until he would be able to fire up his video game console and lose himself in fantastical worlds. But, as it turned out, video games would have to wait.

Something hadn't felt right when Jock had trod into the changing rooms.

Something had been off in the atmosphere.

He soon discovered what it was when he trod into the middle of the changing room. And found himself surrounded.

Henry Foldes.

And his merry band of morons.

Jock had seen the mean expressions spread across their faces and he had known that he had to run. That he should've bolted at the first sign of trouble.

And yet his whole body had gone stiff.

Then he had felt the hands on him — grabbing him from all sides. Before he knew quite what was going on, Jock found himself pinned up against one of the cold changing room walls. When he shut his eyes, he could still see those hardened, *cruel* expressions surrounding him.

Wanting to see ... well, what they were about to see.

Henry Foldes had occupied the centre of Jock's vision from then onward.

In keeping with the track-and-field activities they had been participating in, there were many pieces of equipment lying about. A javelin amongst everything else.

He had believed the stories about Max had been a joke.

That they'd been invented ... *just stories*.

But then, as the mob had forced his PE shorts down, dragged them about his ankles, the truth had struck him.

They hadn't been stories at all.

His vision had started to blur as Henry Foldes had dragged the javelin back, getting as much force as he could muster, and then brought it swinging forward *hard*.

The pain had been indescribable.

Jock could recall a ringing sound in his ears.

A feeling of dizziness striking him.

And then his mind had got away.

He had been aware of the intense warmth between his legs.

No pain ... not yet.

He smelled the coppery scent of blood on the air.

But it was like smelling someone else's blood.

When he came around later, with Mr Blindfield standing over him, asking what had happened, Jock had muttered all he could manage.

That he had *fallen*.

Mr Blindfield took this to mean that Jock had fallen and somehow entangled himself with the javelin.

An unfortunate accident.

And one which had left him bereft of testicles.

As Jock looked himself over in the mirror, he balled his fists down at his thighs.

He had always wondered what it was that drove men to kill, and he couldn't help thinking that it must be a situation such as this one.

Could he kill?

Would that be revenge?

For all of the adult relationships which Jock had been deprived of ... all of those women who had been unable to see beyond his ... *wound*.

Today.

Today he would see.

JOANNE

9.56 AM, SUNDAY

J oanne woke with a smile lining her lips.

It took her a second to recall just where she was ... that she was at home.

That she was *back* home.

Somehow, while she'd been asleep, she'd managed to convince herself that she had stayed the night. That she had plucked up the *guts* to stay the night with Henry.

But, no, she had returned home.

As she recalled further details of the previous night, she brought to mind the tense stand-off she had shared with Elena.

Just *what* had been her problem?

Why had she kept Joanne from leaving?

Asked her if Henry had "hurt" her in some way.

Of course, thinking about it now, Joanne had to admit that he had been a little rough when they had begun, but she had hardly been a snowy white angel herself.

She had been the one to kick up his instincts.

She had been the one to *kiss* him.

She had taken control.

Joanne pushed back her duvet, realising she could hear a reprimanding voice downstairs. As she prodded her feet into the slippers which she had kicked off onto the carpet, she impulsively identified the voice as belonging to her sister.

With a yawn, she rose to her feet. She was still wearing the same clothes she'd been in the night before; she hadn't bothered to get changed for bed.

Sloppy.

Not *particularly* fetching in a lady.

Then again, just who was she *trying* to impress?

For so long during her adolescence, she had tried to impress everyone. She had always done her best to make everyone *like* her.

And where had it got her?

Divorced with two children.

And living with her sister.

Could that be seen as any sort of success?

As she made her way along the landing, and then down the stairs, in the direction of her sister and her girls, she thought about one particular moment the night before which *had* struck her as odd.

After she and Henry had ... *finished* ... they had embraced one another.

In her mind, Joanne had always believed that deferring gratification only made it all the sweeter. And she hadn't been disappointed.

They had gone at one another with a wild passion.

While they had lain together, she had noticed how Henry had become somewhat restless. How he seemed completely unable to remain still. She had wanted to ask him what the problem was, as if it might be something she'd be able to solve. And then she recalled his mother was dying in the very same house where they had just made love.

Wasn't it obvious what had been bothering him?

In the end, as the two of them had lain together, she had felt his fingers lightly tracing the outside of her thigh, before working inward. It had been a reflex which'd led to her reaching out and stopping him.

Preventing him from going any further.

But it was too late.

Already his fingertips had brushed the scar tissue.

And they had halted.

She had expected him to ask about the scar, that since he had spent so much time exploring that area he would be curious to hear the story behind it.

But he had said nothing.

And soon after he had drawn his fingers away.

Joanne had left soon after. She recalled walking through the empty, silent house and then getting on her bike and riding away.

Well, that was *almost* the truth.

She had stopped briefly to examine the stone statue another time.

To look at it *again*.

Still the final time she had seen Henry laid heavy on her mind.

Even now that they'd broken the "tension".

The sitting room was as calamitous as it always was.

Dolls, wood blocks, dress-up clothes strewn all over.

Joanne met her sister Beth's eye as she stood in the doorway.

She knew *that* stare well.

That look of "reproach".

Joanne had been a Bad Girl, and Beth was determined to make her see that.

Beth had *always* been the good one.

Perhaps that was why she'd never had children of her own ... too *well-behaved* ...

Joanne's two daughters, Carla and Lauren, leaped at her.

She hoisted Carla — her two-year-old — up in her arms. She gave a twirl and then brought up Lauren — her five-year-old — so she could treat her in a similar way.

Both girls giggled out of delight.

Soon enough, Joanne found herself facing off with Beth.

God, she *hated* it when Beth chose to do it like this.

Joanne couldn't care less if her sister criticised her, but she did care that her sister did it in front of her girls. She didn't want her girls to grow up thinking that their mother was nothing but a gigantic fuck-up. From the books she'd read, she knew children took in these things on a subconscious level from birth.

"Mummy's going out in a couple of hours," Beth said, in a snide voice.

Joanne wasn't completely sure what to make of this statement. Of course there was truth to it. But Joanne, as she had arranged implicitly with her sister Beth, had announced her intentions more than a month earlier. Sure, she hadn't gone through the same protocol for the meeting which'd taken place last night ... the sudden decision which Elena had taken to bring them all together.

For "revenge".

Joanne still wasn't any clearer *exactly* what Elena even meant by that word.

Exactly what she had in mind.

Or if she had any sort of plan at all.

"You have a good night?" Beth asked, as Joanne let Lauren down.

The girls had been playing with building blocks.

They'd been constructing a pretty sizeable tower before Joanne had interrupted.

"Yes, thank you," Joanne replied.

Beth sighed. "I'll just put my life on hold, then, shall I? While you get through with all these *arrangements* of yours?"

"When it comes time for your school reunion then I'll be perfectly happy to babysit Horace for you."

This was greeted with narrowed eyes.

Horace was Beth's cat.

And, yes, Joanne did make cat-lady jokes on a regular basis.

Joanne looked to her girls, already surprised at how self-reliant they were, how the two of them could pass hours in one another's company making up all sorts of imaginary situations with whichever toys were to hand.

"Cup of tea?" Beth asked, in a sarcastic voice.

Joanne ignored the tone. "Coffee would be better. Please."

Beth sighed again then disappeared into the kitchen. As she went, she called out, "Well don't stand about like a lemon. Go have a shower, get changed. You'll be late."

Joanne thought about this for a moment, and then, looking over her girls and deciding they were doing just fine without her, she did as Beth suggested.

MR BLINDFIELD

11.39 AM, SUNDAY

Alexander Blindfield examined himself in the mirror, straightening the kink out of his tie. Ever since his wife, Fiona, had passed away three years ago he had had to get used to doing his own laundry. He had had to get used to taking care of his own appearance. It hadn't been until about a month after his wife's death — when he had finally returned to his work here; a PE teacher at Saint Camelgal *High School* — that the little details had struck him. How Fiona would lay out his sports clothing the night before. How he would only need to slip on his tracksuit bottoms, zip up his jacket over his crisp, flawlessly ironed white polo shirt. His trainers, too, would always be the same pristine white as his shirt. Now all of those responsibilities had fallen to him.

It was strange.

There had been moments, back when Fiona had been suffering from her illness, in which Alexander had wondered what he would do without her. It ashamed him to admit — even to himself — that the thought had crossed his mind more than once that he might be granted a fresh bout of freedom. That once the thick fog of grief had cleared, he would launch himself into seeking out the company of another.

But, three years later, the urge still hadn't struck him.

It had taken this long to learn how to take care of himself.

It was much harder than he would've imagined.

For one thing, there were the suits he had to wear on occasions such as the annual class reunion today. While these reunions were optional, he quite enjoyed them. He supposed that career teachers, those who were constantly looking to better themselves, to swing from school to school, searching for greater and greater challenges, might've found these reunions to be an obligation they could do without.

Alexander, however, had worked at Saint Camelgal for the entirety of his career.

And he took pleasure in seeing where students ended up.

As this was the year of his retirement he would never work anywhere else.

More than once he had heard himself being described as part of the "fabric" of Saint Camelgal. Although it was slightly corny it never failed to stoke a gentle warm glow of pride in his gut. It was difficult to get his head around the idea he had worked at the same school for over forty years. These days it was a rare feat for a teacher to last beyond two or three years at the same school ... if not in the profession itself.

Alexander put his perceived stamina down to two factors.

Firstly, it was his belief that young people had never had things so easy. Or, if not easy, then at least eas*ier* than it had been at his age. Back when Alexander had considered what he might make his profession, teaching had been a solid career path with a good salary. The rest of his family had been miners. He had always considered himself fortunate that he had possessed a certain flare for football; that same flare which, once a professional career had slipped from view, had at least afforded him an opportunity to teach PE at the local school.

The second factor was more personal.

It was Alexander's belief that because he was a *PE* teacher rather than, say, a chemistry teacher, a maths teacher, or — *shudder* — an English teacher, he was allowed to enjoy himself more.

Whereas, in the classroom, the only tools which teachers had at their disposal to cope with unruly children were raised voices or the threat of extra homework, Alexander could send his students on laps around the field, or else order them to do push-ups in the mud. There was no teacher like good honest exercise.

It was all a matter of putting students in their place.

Alexander backed away from the mirror.

He could hear a pair of voices carrying along the corridor.

He recognised them.

The head and the deputy.

As he watched them stride by the doorway, he couldn't help but think of the presentation that was planned to honour his service to the school that afternoon.

When he looked back in the mirror, he realised a single tear had sneaked down his cheek. He wiped it away with his palm, cleared his throat and straightened his tie.

HENRY

12.06 PM, SUNDAY

Although he would've much preferred to have jumped on a bike, or even walked, it was out of the question. Not after the night Harry had had. Sleep dragged at his eyelids as he guided his car along the narrow streets of Goonherth Bay.

It was an odd experience.

Everything was so familiar. It was a kind of waking dream. He reached the roundabout which led to the school and came to a halt. He gave himself a sharp pinch on the forearm, hoping to stir himself.

To inject some life into his nervous system.

To get his brain *working*.

He brought his car through the open school gates, following the temporary parking signs pointing to the playground. He parked between two other cars and then sat for a moment at the wheel. He breathed the hot air of the car interior, trying to get his head back together. His mind felt stretched. As did his body.

He felt a slight twang at the base of his spine.

It had been a long drive to get here, to Goonherth Bay.

Last night, he had sat up beside his mother until the early morning. He had only stirred when his watch had sounded the alarm he had forgotten to disable.

There was still time — time for him to pull away.

To *go* back home.

To The Crosses.

To his mother.

No one had seen him yet.

And the only person who knew he was coming at all was Joanne.

Why was he here?

... Because Joanne had wanted him to come.

Why was he doing what she wanted? What was so important about her?

... And she had *two children*, for Chrissake!

What was he getting himself tangled up in?

But, however much Harry attempted to reason away his situation, he only succeeded in tying himself up in ever-tightening mental knots.

In the end, muttering a swearword beneath his breath, he slipped out of the car, feeling downtrodden and mucky in the creased suit he had produced from his travelling case. If only his co-workers could see him now, he would get a right ribbing. In his circles, a creased suit was grounds to be suspected as a member of the Great Unwashed.

Harry absorbed his surroundings and decided he was to follow the signs which read "Registration". He fell into step with the scattering of other early-arrivals. As he glanced at their faces, he was struck with that same phantasmal twitch which'd afflicted him on the drive here. That *absurd* feeling of the familiar.

And the alien.

Just like a dream.

... A weird fucking dream.

A bright-eyed young thing took Harry's details.

He watched as she consulted the list of confirmed guests, knowing she wouldn't find his name there. Indeed, when she furrowed her mucky-brown eyebrows at him, he turned on the charm. In the end, it was with a smile, and under his instruction, that she wrote out his name in her neat handwriting and passed him a laminated name badge.

The signs led him to a newly renovated sports hall.

So new he could still smell the chemical stench of freshly installed linoleum.

New pieces of sports kit too:

Folded-up trampolines. Frames of monkey bars. There were cricket nets beyond the rows and rows of blue plastic chairs set out for the reunion. Something of an upgrade compared to his recollections of the school hall. Back when he had been here, there had been several floor tiles missing, not to mention a broken windowpane or three. Kids had it much better these days. Not that they would care much ...

That said, he imagined the sole purpose of school remained the same:

Survival.

Get in.

Get *out*.

No matter what anyone else might think.

MR BLINDFIELD
12.19 PM, SUNDAY

Alexander had believed it would be more difficult to recognise the faces among the crowd. When he had made rough mental calculations he had decided that in his forty years at the school he must've seen no fewer than twenty *thousand* faces.

And yet, he *did* remember several among this year.

Indeed, he could put names to some of those faces.

Perhaps, after all the reunions, Alexander had acquired a knack for seeing the ageing process at work. Maybe he could mentally age a face ... picture how it would look *years* from now. Of course, the face which he recognised above all others was that of Henry "Harry" Foldes.

Despite the school uniform, and all those other measures implemented to strive for "equality" among pupils, Harry Foldes had been undeniably *different*.

Not only had Harry excelled in every area of his studies but he had also been the star player of whichever sports team Alexander saw fit to pick him for. In itself that wasn't something exceptional; indeed it seemed that just about every year there was a standout student who was good at *everything*.

No, there was *something else* about him.

If Alexander had been that way inclined, he might've described it as an "aura".

He had seen it up close and personal. Whenever Harry Foldes would saunter through the corridors, other students would stand reverent, as if he was a god walking among them. Harry Foldes — children of his *means* — were generally far more at home attending Barkmar, the local boarding school.

His parents, however, had elected to send him to the local comprehensive.

Like the rest of the staff, Alexander had heard the stories, of course.

The *rumours*.

And, without proof, that was all they could ever be.

The stories were as sordid as they were *bizarre*.

And from what Alexander had seen personally they seemed totally at odds with the boy he had known. Then again, how well could a teacher ever really know his pupil?

The hall was full now, everyone having found their places.

It was eerie how similar the mannerisms of adults were to those of children when gathered together in a school hall.

The *babble* of chit-chat.

Sneaked glances to the teachers sat up front.

From his experience of school reunions, Alexander well knew that adults wasted little time in locating their former pals. They seemed to slip back into old times as if it had only been yesterday when they had rubbed shoulders. That, he supposed, was one thing he had come to understand over the years.

Twenty years was really no time at all.

Alexander glanced to the head teacher who was shuffling his notes.

The ceremony was about to start.

And Alexander needed to prepare himself.

None of that *blubbing* which'd momentarily afflicted him a little while ago.

No more of *that* ...

But — *God* — how he hated public speaking.

He hated the way his stomach would sink.

He hated the hot and cold flushes.

And he'd silently curse at how he seemed to sweat from every pore as he stumbled over his words. As he struggled against the dyslexia which'd gone undiagnosed until a few years ago. At least he had an excuse. Something to point to. Not that he ever would. Today, like all days, was simply a matter of doing his best.

Just as he was always telling his students.

All you can do is your best.

Straight back, gut pulled in ... *do your best.*

As the head teacher cleared his throat, Alexander drew in a deep breath and pinned on a smile.

MAX

12.26 PM, SUNDAY

I t was near impossible for Max to control his legs.

As he sat in the school hall, feeling the words of the head teacher wash over him like some invisible, gloopy tide, he supposed he was feeling anger. Although he could only see the back of his head, it was enough that the two of them shared the same room:

Henry Foldes.

He supposed he had believed the two of them would never again need to breathe the same air. It seemed now, though, that this belief had been misplaced.

Last night, he had barely been able to sleep.

Anxiety.

Anticipation.

Excitement?

He looked around. Caught Jock's eye.

The two of them were sitting side by side.

When he cast a glance over his shoulder, he saw Joanne and Elena had arrived together. They sat on the back row. Neither so much as glanced at him.

Max forced himself to tune back into the head teacher's words —

he hadn't had time to catch his name. His mind had been fixed on ... *other* matters.

He felt the steady weight of the knife in the inner pocket of his jacket.

This was nothing like those countless TV shows he had watched.

Or the many, many movies.

The knife didn't call out to him. And neither did it speak softly yet insistently into his ear. No, it was more just the knowledge.

The knowledge that it was within reach.

If and when he needed it.

Max looked down at his legs. He forced himself to stop jiggling them.

A regrettable nervous habit.

When he glanced up he saw the head teacher handing a golden statuette to Mr Blindfield in honour of his service. Mr Blindfield stood there, dewy-eyed, bottom lip wobbling. What Max wouldn't give to stick his knife into Henry Foldes.

Today.

JOCK

12.28 PM, SUNDAY

Jock was surprised at how calm he felt.

His therapist had led him through a series of exercises designed to stop him freaking out. One of these exercises had him imagining a desert island.

Searing blue skies.

Bottomless, azure oceans.

Not a soul in sight.

Only *him*.

He sat against a palm tree, feeling its trunk supporting his spine.

He shovelled his bare feet in the fine sand, feeling the grains trickle between his toes. His brain felt as if it might melt from the heat. He thought about nothing but the island. He had escaped.

He switched back onto Mr Blindfield.

Saw him standing before them.

Mr Blindfield had always put Jock in mind of an ape. The fact that he was twenty years older, and wearing a suit, did nothing to diminish this impression.

He was an elderly ape now.

It felt as if all his life Jock had needed to put up with idiots.

Mediocrity.

Even now, twenty years later, he felt the burn of having to take instruction from such no-marks as PE teachers. What had compelled them to one day pop on shorts and bark out orders at kids taking part in compulsory exercise rituals?

What sort of a *weirdo* would ever consider such a career?

In those same therapy sessions, Jock had often found himself speaking about his parents, about their personal attitudes to academic achievement. It was odd to think that — at the time, when he had been younger — he had never really stopped to think about his parents. They had simply been *there*. However, with the aid of his therapist, Jock had succeeded in identifying several key features of his parents which might well have had a gargantuan impact not just on his school life but on everything which'd unfolded afterward.

They hadn't accepted excuses or half measures.

They had set high standards for the world and themselves.

And certainly for their son.

They were *constantly* questioning where their time was being spent.

How their resources were being allocated.

With the therapist, Jock had explored how this attitude had almost certainly led directly to his exemplary marks, and how he had got into a prestigious university. But they had also explored how this attitude had impacted other areas of his life.

Interpersonal relationships mostly.

At school, Jock recalled very clearly the day when he had spoken out of turn, cutting through his physics teacher's explanation to raise a concern that he had contradicted himself, only to be sent from the room for "speaking out of turn".

Ever since that day, Jock had made a point to stay quiet.

To *never* again "speak out of turn".

Jock eyed the bumbling, and possibly senile, man-boy take a step forward:

Mr Blindfield.

He watched on as he fumbled with the index cards he held, searching for his place, no doubt attempting to decipher untidy, childlike handwriting.

A smirk tugged back the corners of Jock's mouth. He supposed it was something of a wonder that the man managed to tie his own shoelaces let alone his necktie.

Had he got the head teacher to lend a helping hand on such a *special* occasion?

Mr Blindfield glanced about the hall. "Uh, ladies and gentle-man," Blindfield began. "I would like to thank Mister Ghorsh ... f-f-for his words of welcome this afternoon. It is ... it is with great plea-sure that I see so many, uh, so many ... so many ... f-familiar *faces*." Blindfield blinked rapidly.

Jock vaguely hoped the man might have an epileptic fit.

That would serve him right.

... How could someone be so *stupid*?

Still clutching his index cards, Blindfield pointed to members of the audience. "Jackie Paulsen, athletics. Adam Gleetarth, football. Uh ... Henry Foldes ... *everything*."

This was greeted by a polite chuckle from the audience and Mr Blindfield raised a nervous, grateful smile in response.

The very name "Harry Foldes" sent a shiver passing up Jock's spine but he held himself still. Did his best to project an outwardly *neutral* image.

Of course Jock had gone over what'd happened That Day with his therapist.

The *injustice* of it all.

"They" had decided that dwelling on the past would only cause harm.

That some things could never be changed.

It was best to forgive, if not forget ...

Very reasonable.

It sounded like something his parents might say.

Blindfield broke off his awestruck gaze directed at Henry Foldes, switching his attention back to the audience at large.

For the briefest of moments, Jock's eyes crossed Blindfield's.

And Blindfield took a sharp breath.

Was that an acknowledgement ... or was it just a coincidence?

When Blindfield continued, his voice was surer, more confident. He was growing into the occasion. "As some of you may already know, this shall be my final year at Saint Camelgal. I wish to thank all of you for being a part of my career. Whenever I look back at ... at my career, it is always my students I think about first of all. Everything I ever did was for my students." There was an odd pause, Blindfield's mouth remained latched open, as if he had something else to add. In the end, a dry, half-gargle escaped his lips.

Jock realised Blindfield was smothering a sob.

Finally, Blindfield found his voice, "... Thank you."

The head teacher began to clap.

And the rest of the hall followed.

With a forced smile and an arthritic bow, Blindfield backed away from the audience's gaze.

The head teacher, Ghorsh, took centre stage and swept through a speech which was about as uninspiring as Jock had expected it to be. When he was through, Ghorsh clapped his hands together as if to bring the audience out of a trance, and said, "without further ado I would like to invite you all outside to take full advantage of this *wonderful* Indian summer we are having. Let the reminiscences commence!"

A couple of polite chuckles among the audience in response to this half-joke.

As people began to get up from their seats, Jock remained sitting.

He wanted to stay here as long as he could manage.

He didn't want to take a trip down Memory Lane.

He wanted something far more pressing.

He wanted *revenge*.

ELENA

12.45 PM, SUNDAY

"Good speech, I thought," Joanne said.

Elena turned her head to Joanne, remembering she was sitting beside her. Finally, she managed to catch herself. "Uh ... yeah," she replied.

"Shall we ..."

Elena glanced about, realising everybody was rising up out of their seats, that they were all headed for the exits, as the head teacher had indicated.

Joanne rose.

Elena followed her cue, breaking off her focus on Jock.

As the two of them slipped into the audience streaming out of the hall, Elena felt herself struck by a strange combination of nostalgia and reluctance. It was such a weird thing — to see all of her school mates together, all of these years later. For some reason, she had believed these people had ceased to exist; that she had succeeded in banishing them from her memory merely by removing her day-to-day interactions with them.

But she was mistaken.

These people had never truly left her mind.

They continued to lurk.

In the depths.

Remembering herself — how she had noticed Jock looking thoroughly *riled* by the whole experience — she looked through the crowd for him.

Her heart skipped a beat.

She couldn't locate him anywhere.

Max neither.

She turned into Joanne, finding her gentle smile completely at odds with the current situation.

Didn't Joanne realise what it was that Elena had started?

Didn't Joanne *realise* just what they might've stirred up and let *loose?*

Then again, Joanne had never really known Henry Foldes.

She had never *known* him like Elena, Max and Jock had.

Outside, sunshine was streaming down.

She could taste the sea air.

Hear the *cackle* of gulls.

Back when she'd been a girl, she had often imagined that the whole of Goonherth Bay was a world apart ... an island just floating in the middle of the sea.

For the remoteness of the place, it might as well have been an island.

And when she had left it behind it had felt *just like* an island.

But now she was back ...

People cropped up on all sides.

On impulse, Elena brought her arms up to cover her chest as if a chill had entered the air. At the same time, she felt the sun beaming down on her shoulders, warming her blood. But this sunlight was different to the summer sun; it didn't have the same effect of stripping away her fears and anxieties. Instead it felt more like a dark, handsome stranger, beckoning her away.

Beckoning her into his *warmth*.

Into his *danger*.

Winter was coming.

There was no doubt about that.

Elena was glad to feel Joanne's sure touch — to feel Joanne loop her arm through her elbow and guide her through the crowds to the table which'd been erected on the school playing field. The table was covered with a white cloth and on top there was an assortment of drinks:

Champagne, beer, wine.

Anything that a reluctant time traveller might want to soothe her nerves.

It was more because of Joanne's insistence than any true urge that saw Elena ending up with a flute of champagne entwined in her fingers. The two of them shifted away onto the playing fields where the rest of their school year had gathered.

Elena felt a fresh tingle in her gut.

She had spotted Max and Jock.

The two of them together.

Neither one attempting to make conversation with the passers-by.

And neither one attempting conversation with the other.

Before Elena had the chance to make up her mind — to decide to go over and see them or to back off; to downplay this so-called "revenge" she had planned — she felt someone standing nearby. Someone with their eyes fixed upon her.

Sure enough, when she turned, she saw a familiar face there.

It took Elena several heartbeats before she truly absorbed what it meant.

The wild blond hair.

Tufty, dark eyebrows.

An angular, triangular — *handsome* — jawline.

Someone of *high breeding* ... or, at least, higher breeding than Elena.

Jasmine Everglade.

Henry Foldes's ex-girlfriend.

His school sweetheart.

Whatever the going definition was ...

Jasmine only cast the most superficial of glances in Elena's direction before shifting onto Joanne. She broke into a wide smile. Showing off row upon row of naturally beautiful teeth. "Jo!" Jasmine cried, throwing her arms about Joanne's neck.

Just before she fell beneath Jasmine's embrace, Elena caught a glimpse of Joanne's expression. She saw the momentary hesitation soon smothered in Jasmine's arms.

Elena tightened her arms about her chest, squeezing herself.

She took a step back from the couple, leaving them to their reminiscences.

When they had got through with their greeting, their joint gaze fell upon her.

It was unpleasant to feel herself transported back to school. To think about how these best of friends would often make her feel an outsider.

As if she was worth less than nothing.

On reflection, Elena couldn't help but wonder if it wouldn't have been better if the two of them had picked on her more directly. At school, all they would do was exclude her. Pretend she didn't even exist. Elena could still recall the momentary satisfaction she'd experienced when Henry Foldes had laid hands on her.

How Elena had *believed* she had one-upped Jasmine somehow.

God, she'd *really* been a fool.

The only one who had come out of the situation winning was Henry Foldes.

Another conquest for him.

Another notch in the bedpost.

What had Elena been thinking?

"It's ... *good* to see you too, El," Jasmine finally said, her focus stopping just before the tip of Elena's nose.

Elena was glad she had no need to reply, because they were interrupted by another sinisterly familiar face.

The reddish-brown, swept-back hair.

And the tall, muscular frame.

Edward Wanton.

One of Henry Foldes's inner circle; for want of a better term.

"*Guten Nachmittag*," he said, glancing between them the same way a wolf might size up a trio of sheep separated from the flock. "Just flown in — from *Berlin*."

As Elena took him in, she couldn't help thinking that Edward looked *so* much as he had done as a boy. He had retained his boyish good looks, not to mention his muscles.

He jerked his thumb over his shoulder as if to indicate the European continent behind him. "Working in diplomatic relations," he said, then rolled his eyes. "Bit *jet-set*, really. Always off this place, or that place."

Elena studied him.

Edward had always been a champion bullshitter.

Back when they had been kids, he had lied about everything and anything.

Edward held his hand up to his eyes, shielding them from the sun as he looked across the playing field. "Either of you seen Harry? Did he come after all?"

Elena finally broke out of her daze. "Why 'after all' ?"

Edward squinted at Elena as if he didn't recognise her.

And as if she should have requested permission before speaking.

"Oh, I spoke with him a few months back — didn't seem all that keen, though he was occupied at the time ... sounded as if he was very *busy*." He shrugged. "Probably forgot all about it, to be honest. About the phone call, I mean."

Edward flinched slightly when he made the last comment.

Was that a tic of some sort?

Giving away a lie?

... But if it was *why* would he lie about something so *trivial*?

Then again, did compulsive liars abide by any sort of creed or code?

Elena noticed how Jasmine looked off across the playing fields as if she hoped to conjure Henry out of thin air. When her gaze crossed Jasmine's, Elena took a sip from the flute of champagne she held.

The bubbles fizzed on her tongue.

Edward's eyes settled upon Elena, her champagne.

His eyes bulged from their sockets.

"Where's the *booze?*" he asked.

Elena nodded him in the right direction.

With a grin, Edward slipped away.

Jasmine, also grinning, set off after him. But not without a few words over her shoulder. "Look forward to catching up later."

Elena watched the pair depart.

Joanne touched her on the shoulder. "What?" Joanne said. "What's the matter?"

"What do you mean?"

Joanne wrinkled her forehead. "That look on your face. Like you've smelled something horrible."

Elena thought about bringing up that which had bothered her throughout their adult-world friendship. Despite everything, she had never so much as uttered a word about how Jasmine and Joanne had been responsible for, if not making her life a misery then making it more unpleasant than it needed to be. And, of course, she had never said anything about *that* night with Henry Foldes.

Might the time be approaching?

Could she afford to allow Joanne into such intimate details?

... Could she *really* trust her?

Elena pressed on a smile and took a few steps across the grass. "Come on," she said. "Let's see what's happened to the hockey pitch."

Frowning, Joanne eyed her a few seconds longer then followed.

JASMINE
1.07 PM, SUNDAY

Jasmine Everglade perused the options available to her at the drinks table.

Champagne.

Beer.

Wine.

All had a habit of going to her head. She had made that resolution all those years ago that she would give up drinking — among other things — for good. And then she had gone ahead and broken that same resolution thousands of times.

She was going to break that resolution all over again.

It had been an event in her late-teens which'd turned her off alcohol; one of those weekends which had been sold to her by her agent as a make-or-break for her fledgling modelling career. All she needed to do was impress at the party. All she needed to do was *put on a show* ... and, well, in a way that was certainly what she had done ...

She could still recall herself down on her knees, hurling her guts out into the swimming pool in the early hours of the morning.

Her dress ruined.

Her shoes ruined.

Her *career* ruined ... shortly after.

And all before it'd even got off the ground.

Edward held up a bottle of beer, offering it to her.

Not thinking, she nodded.

He gave her a disbelieving glare.

She couldn't help but smile in response.

After all this time he still knew her. "Make it wine, then."

Jasmine observed the woman tending the drinks table. She was in her mid-to-late thirties. About Jasmine's age. A teacher or a parent? She was a youngish woman, her hair cropped just below the chin. If only she allowed her hair to grow a couple of inches it might mitigate her podgy cheeks. And grant her a little more *sex* appeal.

Then again, as Jasmine accepted the glass of red wine Edward handed to her, she supposed that teachers weren't supposed to devote themselves to such matters.

Their motives were far more noble.

They existed to *educate*.

"Want to mingle?" Edward asked.

Jasmine felt her stomach sink slightly.

To tell the truth, she hadn't much been anticipating this reunion.

She had believed it would bring nothing but depressing thoughts.

Even Elena Kardos — for *goodness' sake!* — looked as if she had made something of herself. She looked well. And better-looking than Jasmine remembered.

"Hang about," Edward said, leaning into her. "You'll never guess who it is."

Jasmine's stomach sank lower still.

She followed Edward's finger.

Henry Foldes.

Well, it was *bound* to happen. If she was going to run into him then why wouldn't it be *here* ... at a school reunion?

At the back of her mind she knew that she had wanted to see him.

Something had drawn her back to Goonherth Bay.

She realised now that it had been Henry Foldes.

Jasmine followed Edward, paying close attention to where she stepped.

For better or worse she had decided on high heels for the occasion. It was a good thing the weather had been so fine the past few weeks — the ground was hard-baked.

For the longest time, Jasmine bowed her head, not wanting to meet his eye without being prepared. But just when would she be prepared?

As they drew near, Edward said, in a lowered voice, "Knew he'd crop up eventually — *knew* he wouldn't be able to stay away."

Jasmine could only raise the slightest — the most *superficial* — of smiles.

For all extents and purposes, Henry was just as she remembered him.

Those wavy, blond curls.

The peachy, innocent-seeming cheeks.

And the deep-blue eyes.

She remembered *those* eyes well.

They had pinned her to the spot *so* many times.

She could still recall trembling in pleasure as she stared into those eyes.

Once Henry Foldes had seemed to encompass her present and future.

But now he was only her past.

Their eyes crossed.

Henry smirked.

And then, as if it was the most natural thing to do after twenty years — *twenty years!* — he planted a kiss on each of her cheeks.

When he drew back, Jasmine felt herself trembling all over once again.

She stared into his eyes, searching for anything to suggest a stirring of his emotions. But she could see nothing at all.

Did he have a wife now?

Children?

... A family?

His voice was as cool and crisp as she remembered.

"It's been a long time, Jazz," he said. "Too long."

How could Jasmine do anything but agree?

MR BLINDFIELD

1.19 PM, SUNDAY

The afternoon sunlight brought a healthy glow out of Alexander's cheeks.

There was a gentle, fresh breeze blowing in off the Atlantic, too.

He felt much better now it was all over — that he had got through with his "speech". He felt the cool bottle of beer in his hand, the alcohol throttling through his veins. The PE teacher in him couldn't help but think about the calories the beer contained, and how long he would need to run in order to burn them off.

"Excuse me?"

Alexander turned.

Absorbed the individual standing before him.

Like the other alumni attending he wore a suit and tie.

Alexander scanned the gaunt face, the stringy black hair which hung down at the sides of his face. He attempted to decipher something ... something he might *recognise*.

Was there a spark?

Some reminiscence?

Or was he just fooling himself?

In the end, Alexander didn't need to rack his brain.

"Jock," the man said. "Jock *Jones*."

Alexander felt a chill pass over the surface of his skin.

His heart skipped one beat. And then another.

A tension gripped his chest.

He tried not to pay attention — just like all those other times.

He would be just fine if he ... if he could just ...

A light-headed sensation struck him.

Alexander took convulsive breaths.

It required almost all his effort to stand up straight.

Jock Jones stuck out his hand for Alexander to shake giving Alexander a much-needed focal point. His grip was much stronger than he could've imagined.

As a boy, Jock had been lanky, unsubstantial physically.

When Jock allowed his hand to slip free of his fingers, Alexander took another few moments to compose himself. He waited for his heart to resume its normal rhythm.

And then looked Jock in the eye.

"It's been a long time," Jock said. "An *awfully* long time."

Alexander felt a single bead of sweat break free of his hairline.

It rolled down his cheek, reaching his chin where it clung.

Alexander summoned a smile from somewhere. "Yes ... it has."

Jock held his gaze. "I wanted to speak with you. Something on my *mind*."

"Oh?" Alexander replied, flashing his eyebrows.

As if he had no idea what Jock was talking about.

"Listen," Jock said, leaning in closer. "I have some questions. About *that* day."

Alexander flinched and then brought his beer bottle to his lips to try and cover the reaction. "Ah, I see ... and what ... day would that be?"

"You know perfectly well."

Alexander did.

And yet it seemed cruel to bring up something from twenty years ago.

Something for which Alexander was legally entirely blameless for.

"You were the first to see," Jock said. "The first to see me, bleeding on the floor."

Again, Alexander flinched.

He needed to get a hold on himself.

This was a drawback of these reunions.

Inevitably, some of the alumni overindulged.

Inhibitions were lowered.

And uncomfortable truths were brought to light.

"Yes," Alexander replied. "That's right. The first ... first to see ... the *accident* ..."

Jock snorted a laugh.

Jock had no drink in his hand — but that didn't mean he hadn't already indulged.

Alexander had to take care.

He glanced about.

Saw the head teacher conversing with a group nearby.

It wouldn't be any great feat to call for help if he needed it.

If this turned out to be something he couldn't handle.

"You and I know," Jock said.

Alexander turned his full attention back to him. "What ... what do we know?"

"We *know*," Jock continued, "that Henry Foldes, and his merry bunch of idiots, did ... did ..." Here he broke off ... his head bowed to his chest.

Alexander realised the two of them were looking at Jock's crotch.

Alexander recovered himself.

Tilted his bottle back once more.

Felt the beer bubble at the back of his throat.

"I want to know ... *why*."

Alexander swallowed.

He saw the head teacher had broken away from the group.

They exchanged glances.

Alexander's lips parted ... and there was a moment ... a moment when he could've called out for help ... but then someone distracted the head teacher and the opportunity was gone. He turned back to Jock. "W-why ... why what?"

Jock's stare was searing. "Why you did nothing — why you protected him. Why you protected Henry Foldes."

Alexander pressed his lips tightly together.

Smirking, Jock sniffed and stared at the ground. "It's okay. Give me an answer later. I want you to think about it. Thinking must be a taxing thing for a mind like yours."

Before Alexander had time to consider a reply to this slight, Jock sauntered off.

He watched him make for the drinks table.

When Alexander went for another sip of beer, he realised the bottle was empty.

Perhaps he could do with a drink himself.

HENRY

1.34 PM, SUNDAY

Harry had promised himself that he wouldn't indulge in alcohol today.

Goodness knew, he had drunk enough the previous day with his father ...

However, when he had been offered a flute of champagne, he had been unable to resist. And, to be quite honest, after the initial hesitation, he didn't regret his choice.

The bubbles tickled his throat and warmed his blood.

They complimented this unseasonably warm September afternoon nicely.

It was surreal for Harry to find himself in the company of Edward and Jasmine on the school playing field. Just to look at the grass brought back memories.

He couldn't help but think about the many football, rugby and cricket matches he had been involved in during his school days. Although he knew the games should've been nothing more than quickly forgotten diversion, he could still recall various and varied details. He could remember specific goals, or tries, or wickets.

Strange that it should all come back to him — that there was some part of his brain which was apparently dedicated to such useless nostalgia.

As he had been speaking with Jasmine and Edward, Harry had noticed his old PE teacher, Mr Blindfield ... or *Alexander* as he supposed he should refer to him now.

He had been conversing with a man Harry hadn't recognised.

What the two of them had spoken about, Harry hadn't a clue, but the way the man stalked away from the scene struck him as odd. As did the bemused expression on Mr Blindfield's face. Harry turned back to Edward, contentedly blabbing away about something or other.

"... And then, when I arrived in Taipei, you should've *seen* the size of them!"

Here Edward made a lewd gesture, insinuating large breasts with wide open arms.

Harry politely sniffed a laugh before turning his attention back to the crowd surrounding them. He could still feel Jasmine's gaze locked on him, of course. He could tell she was staring at him intently.

That she wanted him to pay attention to *her*.

Hadn't that always been the way?

... Hadn't that *always* been the problem in their relationship?

In the end, Harry couldn't understand how he had managed to bear her for so long.

Sensing that Edward was wrapping up his stories — his eyes damp with tears, barely able to contain his laughter — Harry turned back to his schoolmates. He pressed on his very best professional smile — the one responsible for so many done deals.

The physical manifestation of "charisma".

"So, Haz," Edward said, "what've you been doing with yourself?"

Harry breathed in deeply, thinking things through.

He mumbled a brief job description, about his place in Islington.

And then he jabbered something or other about his "lifestyle".

How it was wonderful.

Once-in-a-lifetime.

So busy he hardly had time to look around.

Even at the assorted exotic locales he visited on work trips.

Jasmine and Edward hung on his every word as he knew they would.

All "charisma" meant was that people wanted to be close to you.

Content didn't matter.

What you *said* didn't matter.

It was enough just to *be* ...

In more self-reflective moments, Harry couldn't help but wonder if his career wasn't just a whole sequence of *fake* acts.

Yes, that was it.

He was a professional *fraud*.

And yet, from what he had learned over the past decade or so, professional frauds made the world go around. Professional frauds greased the wheels. They set everything spinning slickly ready to fall apart at any moment but somehow just holding together.

Realising he had said everything he could say about his job, Harry looked over Jasmine and Edward again. He wondered if he should say something about his mother, about how she was at death's door, and how he was wasting his time *here* at some dumb school reunion. But Harry had never believed that friends were for confiding in. Friends were little more than props; a means for people to visually gauge someone's value.

It was when Jasmine began to speak about modelling — or something — that Harry noticed her:

Joanne Darkly.

Her arm threaded through another woman's.

And, before he knew it, he was being swept away.

Back to *that* night ... the night which had changed everything.

The night that had changed *him*.

"... Harry? Harry?"

Caught in a daze, Harry turned his attention back to Jasmine. Although she wore a smile, there was a sharpness in her eye. A sense of imminent danger. That she might not be too far away from grabbing hold of his balls and tearing them loose of his scrotum.

Even that jealous passion had worn thin after a while — in the same way that someone living in a tornado might become tired of constantly twirling around ...

"Can I get you something else to drink?" she asked.

Harry glanced down at his glass. He had already drunk his champagne.

Yes, the slight buzz through his mind was testament to that.

Glad to be shot of her for at least a few minutes, Harry passed his empty glass to her. Their hands brushed for a fraction of a second. She gave him one of her sly, secretive smiles. A smile which did nothing for him.

And then — mercifully — she was gone.

Harry was free to fix his attention back on Joanne as she trod through the crowd.

The woman with her looked familiar.

Well, this *was* a school reunion so most likely she would be.

What Harry *wouldn't* do to be alone with Joanne.

For the two of them to be alone together *again* ... to have *that* night again ...

Another chance.

ELENA

1.58 PM, SUNDAY

As Elena found her way through the strangely familiar — and yet *utterly changed* — school corridors to the toilets, she realised she was having a bit of trouble walking straight. It didn't feel as if she'd had that much to drink. She had had a glass of wine, and then another ... had she really had *three*? ... Or was her mind playing tricks on her?

The toilets had a transparent corrugated plastic roof which allowed sunlight to stream in and which also heated up the room to an oppressive temperature. As she stepped into the enclosed space, she smelled bleach mixed with urine and other odours.

She slipped into one of the cubicles, taking her time in padding the seat with a generous layer of toilet paper. It seemed almost an unsightly waste for only a few seconds of peeing but needs must ...

Leaving, she heard a low, gravelly voice coming from the male toilets.

She flirted with the idea of continuing on her way.

Of venturing back out onto the playing field.

But she stopped short.

It sounded like someone in distress.

Elena sauntered up to the doorway to the male toilets, and then, hearing the groan reach a new level of loudness, she said, "Is everything all right in there?" She paused, waiting for a response. "Do you need any help?"

Still no reply from within.

Should she back off?

She held her ground.

And heard another groan.

This time she decided she had to do something.

She stepped into the toilets.

Just as with the women's toilets, there was that overwhelming stench of bleach mixed in with human excrement. She vaguely wondered if there was anything more distinctive — anything more *off-putting* — than the stink of a school toilet.

She glanced about the urinals, establishing right away that there was no one peeing there. Next she shifted her attention to the only closed cubicle.

The groaning still sounded.

Elena hesitated, wondering if she might be putting herself in danger.

But she forced herself onward.

Arriving just outside the cubicle door, she asked, "Can I help you with anything? Do you *need* anything?"

This time there was a groan louder than anything which had come before.

It cut through her eardrums.

Rattled her heart about her ribcage.

Everything within her told her to back away.

And yet she remained fixed on the cubicle.

Determined to help if she could.

When she spoke again, her voice shook. "If you open the door I might be able to help." She paused, half anticipating there would be another one of those repulsive shrieking groans. She reached down for the cubicle lock.

She knew the tricks, of course. Anyone who had attended Saint Camelgal or any other school knew the master key for all the toilet cubicles was a fifty pence piece.

Elena produced the coin, slotted it in the lock, and said, "I'm coming in."

She hesitated another second and then, hearing no protests, opened the door.

Elena was prepared for all manner of things.

An older member of staff struggling.

Or someone swept up with some sort of grief.

Or just someone suffering through the kind of personal pain which a school reunion raked up. All those memories better left alone.

A fully-dressed man sat slumped on the closed toilet seat.

His eyes were shut.

His cheeks had gone blue.

Oh God, was he *breathing*?

Elena grabbed hold of his shirt.

Shook him.

"Hello? Hello? Can you hear me? *Hello!*"

The man didn't respond.

There was nobody obviously nearby.

What should she do?

She had taken a first-aid course back when she'd been a teenager ... but she doubted that would serve her here.

She turned back to the man, her mind skittering along.

Tried to bring her thoughts clear.

As she absorbed the man's appearance, she realised who it was:

Edward Wanton.

One of Henry's cronies.

She had seen him about an hour earlier.

He had looked fine then.

Thinking quickly, Elena spoke his name out loud. "Edward? *Edward?!*"

His eyelids twitched open a fraction.

She slapped him on the cheek.

She did so again.

And again.

This time his eyelids fluttered open.

His lips parted.

He mumbled something but Elena couldn't make it out.

"Come on," she said, easing him more upright on the toilet seat. "You need to help me — let's get you sitting up straight, okay?"

Although Edward said nothing, he did help her.

His body was no longer limp — impossible for her to lift on her own.

She propped him up against the cistern and he didn't flop over and crash onto the floor. Once she'd got him sitting up straight, he blabbered something else.

"What?" Elena said. "I can't ... I don't *understand* you ..."

Edward was staring at a spot on the floor.

She followed his gaze.

Saw what occupied his attention.

A syringe.

Its needle smeared with blood.

The glass vial empty.

Plunger depressed.

Elena just stared.

Then she broke away.

A rivulet of blood ran down the inside of Edward's arm, where he had punctured the vein. "What is it?" she asked. "What've you put up your arm?"

Edward just blabbered again.

Tentatively, Elena took a step back.

Edward remained propped up against the cistern, not flopping over. His eyeballs lolled beneath his half-closed lids. His whole body rocked from side to side, but he seemed more or less stable for the time being.

"Wait here," Elena said, as if he was going to do anything else.

It wasn't until she reached the doorway when she heard his voice bark out.

It sent a shudder down her spine.

A *flashback* ... something like that.

She pushed it away from her mind.

Turned back to him.

Saw he had somehow found his feet.

And that he had staggered to the cubicle door.

He was leaning heavily against it.

Tears streamed down his cheeks.

His complexion was a bloody red.

When he spoke, though, his words were clear, unambiguously stated.

"Don't bring ... anyone," he said, and then, calmer this time, clearly getting a better hold on his surroundings, the situation, "Don't bring anyone, El."

She could never recall Edward calling her "El" ... or even addressing her at all.

He had been the enemy.

One of the enemies.

She had only been convenient prey.

"Stay," he said, finally. "Stay with me."

His speech was more lucid now.

He was coming around ... from whatever it was that he was coming around *from*.

Elena hovered in the doorway.

Thinking through her options.

JOANNE
2.11 PM, SUNDAY

C louds had begun to roll in.

What had once been a pleasant breeze now had a chilly bite to it.

Since the sunlight had dimmed, and shadows had begun to stretch out, the playing field had taken on an unreal quality. As if the colour had been washed out of the lush green grass. The once-golden leaves on the trees had turned a dull bronze. The chirping laughter around her had become much more sedate.

She felt antsy.

Elena had gone off about fifteen minutes ago.

And there was still no sign of her.

She wondered if she should go and check on her.

In the end, she decided against it.

As far as Joanne knew, Elena had run into an old flame, and the two of them were having a "good time" in some illicit corner. Who this theoretical "old flame" might be, Joanne had no idea. She and Elena hadn't been friends at school and even now that they were best friends in the "adult" world they barely mentioned those times.

As if they hadn't happened at all.

"Well, when're you gonna say hello?"

Joanne turned.

Henry Foldes.

Harry.

She took in the blond curls.

The sly smile fixed on his pert, angelic mouth.

It was hard to believe what had happened the previous night.

That the two of them had ... *shared* one another.

On the other hand, it had seemed inevitable. Something which had been put off for so long but which, now it was done with, could finally be buried.

Joanne had only to imagine what her sister Beth would say about her taking in Henry Foldes as her beau ...

Beth would probably go ahead and call Child Services herself.

No, Henry Foldes was not the marrying kind. He was the sort of man who would be a constant source of excitement in the bedroom, and in other places ... whenever he decided to come home, that was.

"I ... didn't see you arrive," Joanne replied.

"No — I suppose I've always been sly like that."

Joanne could tell Harry hadn't slept well.

She couldn't blame him.

If one of her own parents had been at death's door, she would've struggled too. She would've stayed up all night by their side. Seeing if there was anything to be done.

If she could — *somehow* — halt the inevitable march of time.

Despite his tiredness, there was a sparkle in Harry's eye. He cut a wide grin and then swooped into her, planting a kiss on either cheek..

"Wonderful to see you here, Jo ... after all these years."

It took Joanne a couple of moments to twig.

Harry was playing.

She switched her mind to the matter at hand. "Yes," she replied, smiling back at him, beginning to blush a little. "It's funny how the years just ... *fly* by."

"Might I be able to buy you a drink?"

"Why," Joanne replied, striking an aristocratic tone, "I shouldn't like to *refuse*."

As Harry led her in the direction of the drinks table, Joanne shot off one final glance in the direction of the toilets, wondering if she might see Elena emerge.

But there was no sign of her.

She was a big girl now ...

JASMINE

2.20 PM, SUNDAY

Jasmine felt her heart beating against the underside of her throat.

A searing-hot sensation had entered her blood.

As the clouds had rolled in overhead, she had felt the air grow thicker.

Clammier.

A feeling akin to claustrophobia.

Not enough *space* ...

She drew her arms about her more tightly, hoping to guard against the chill on the breeze. She could do with another drink.

That would do the trick.

Although he had hardly been *diamond* company, when Edward had slipped away he had left her standing all alone. And Jasmine *hated* to be alone.

It felt like everyone at the reunion was sneaking glances at her.

Leaning into one another.

Asking *why* Jasmine Everglade was alone.

She saw Henry Foldes at the drinks table.

Her heart skipped a beat.

And then her stomach sank.

Because she saw who he was with.

Joanne.

Joanne *Darkly*.

God, what Jasmine wouldn't do to be done with that *bitch*.

For almost a year, Jasmine had been lovesick when Henry had finally cut her off — when he had decided that he needed "room to breathe". And although she had never been able to say for certain that Joanne Darkly was the object of Henry's *distracted* affections, it seemed the only reason for his dimming attraction to her.

And here they were now.

The two of them smiling away.

"Having a drink".

It was enough to make Jasmine *sick*.

What did Joanne have that Jasmine didn't?

Was it because she had always played up to that choirgirl image of hers?

Because she had always presented herself as purer than *pure*?

Of course Joanne knew that there had been others — that was one of the unspoken conditions of Jasmine and Henry's relationship — and while Henry would often speak of his conquests with Jasmine, and how they were infinitely inferior to her, he had never once spoken of Joanne.

And that had meant only one of two things:

That he had never slept with Joanne.

Or that he *had* slept with her, but chosen not to share the details with Jasmine.

Had she just been a fool?

Was that the simple truth?

Was she an idiot to believe she was anything more to Henry Foldes than an "easy fuck"? It certainly seemed so to judge from how he had treated her this afternoon.

To how he had been so distracted.

Well, at least Jasmine knew now *why* he had been distracted.

Jasmine continued to watch Henry and Joanne walk together, each bearing a glass of wine. She tracked them as they trod toward the school building — heading for the hall. The reason why they were doing so only struck Jasmine after several seconds.

When she noticed other alumni following on their heels.

Raindrops were falling.

She felt them streak her cheeks.

Land on her exposed forearms.

She broke out of her daze, forcing herself to follow the others.

Perhaps she should just leave.

That would be the sensible thing to do.

But first she wanted to be sure.

Absolutely sure.

MAX
2.26 PM, SUNDAY

As Max headed for the men's toilets, he realised he could hear voices.

Voices and the gentle sound of footsteps.

On instinct, because he was a polite person, he turned side-on to let whoever was coming pass by. He was taken somewhat by surprise when he absorbed Elena's familiar face, and surprised even further when he recognised the person accompanying her.

Even after all these years he recognised *that* face.

Edward Wanton.

Max remembered Edward Wanton *very clearly indeed*.

Edward Wanton had held the door to the chemistry lab shut while Henry had poured the acid ... down *there*.

Max could still hear Edward's overexcited, childish laughter ringing in his ears.

Even these years later, Max held Edward just as responsible.

Right now Edward was sweating profusely. His eyes were red-raw.

Neither of them noticed him as they passed by.

But that was fine. Max was used to not being noticed.

When Max got through with using the urinal, and he was alone with the mirror he looked himself in the eye. It *really* was him who stared back.

He still felt the steady weight of the flick knife concealed within the inside pocket of his suit jacket. It would be so easy for him to whip it out, to chase after Edward, and to bring him down. To bring him to his *knees*.

But that would only serve as a warning.

It would give Henry Foldes the chance to escape.

And, more than anything else, Max was determined *not* to allow Henry Foldes to escape. Not now that he had him this close. Not when he had the chance to make him *pay* for what he had done.

Max heard more footsteps.

They were steady.

Controlled.

So unlike how he felt right now.

When he glanced up, he saw a familiar face.

Jock.

The two of them exchanged nods, as Max splashed water on the insides of his wrists, hoping to cool his seething, brutally hot blood.

They hadn't been friends at school, although Max didn't quite understand why. Since neither one of them had had any friends their lives would surely have only been improved if they'd taken one another in. And yet it hadn't seemed an option at the time.

There was an odd, unchangeable quality about school.

That, Max supposed, was what had most frightened him about those days. Once you slipped into routine — once you knew who your friends were — things would not change for the five years of schooling to come. It was already set in stone.

When Jock emerged from the cubicle the two of them exchanged glances.

Max thought that Jock was about to say something, but instead he simply bowed his head to the basin and splashed his face with cold water. Finished, Jock took a few steps towards the exit. Max reached out and snatched hold of his suit lapels.

The two of them eyeballed one another.

Max's heart throbbed at his temple.

He waited for Jock's response.

He almost made himself believe Jock would fight back.

That there would be a survival mentality just beneath the surface.

Ready to bite back.

But Jock remained limp.

Max spoke. "What's the plan? What's Elena's plan?"

Jock held still.

Never leaving Max's gaze.

"Doesn't seem like she has one, does it?" Jock replied.

Max nodded off in the direction of the corridor. "Seems to be getting nice and cosy with that twat Wanton."

"Mm."

"You think we can trust her?"

" 'Trust her' with what?"

"Revenge."

Max studied Jock's expression for the longest time.

Even though he was staring into Jock's eyes, he wouldn't have liked to speculate what the exact thoughts were which pumped through his head. That was one thing which would always remain unknowable. There was never any way to say for sure just what someone else was thinking about. Slowly, because it seemed right, Max slipped the flick knife from the inside pocket of his suit jacket.

Jock's eyes widened as he took in the knife.

For the first time, Max sensed pure fear.

He knew that emotion well.

When Jock finally did speak, it was in response to an unvoiced question.

But Max thought he understood all the same.

"Okay," Jock said.

Gradually, Max allowed the knife to drop down to his side.

He nodded back.

The two of them left the men's toilets together.

MR BLINDFIELD
5.55 PM, SUNDAY

Alexander staggered through the playground car park.

Raindrops rattled down upon his umbrella.

He watched as they collected into rivulets and poured down onto the already soaked cement. The skies were grisly grey. The air had a *really* biting chill to it now. It was difficult to believe that this morning golden sunshine had beamed down across the entirety of the landscape. Now it had been replaced by nondescript *murk*.

Autumn had finally arrived. A line drawn beneath the summer. It would be all rugby and football from here on out; no more cricket until springtime.

He eyed his car — a boxy, ten-year-old hatchback — and dug about within his jacket pocket for the fob. He jabbed the button, making the hazard lights flash and heard the staccato *click-click* as the locks disengaged.

With a slightly sleepy sigh, he approached the driver's side.

Over his shoulder, he could still hear babbling voices from the school hall.

The reunion had been slated to run from midday until six o'clock in the evening. However, as he knew from past experience, they would often go on for much longer.

For the first of the reunions, he had stayed behind. It was somewhat otherworldly to converse with people who had once been his students. Over the course of the last few years, though, he had found his stamina waning. And he had seemed less and less capable of drinking as much as he once had. He knew if he didn't make a point of going home now — of getting himself tucked up in bed relatively early — then he would *really* be paying for it on Monday, tomorrow, when school was back in session. He had more young minds to impress with ... well, whatever "wisdom" he had to impart ...

With that thought he slipped into the driver's seat.

He hesitated a moment, padding his jacket, searching for the car keys.

After about a minute of searching, he saw he'd allowed them to drop into his lap.

He swore to himself — something about *going senile*.

Finally, he stuck the key in the appropriate slot.

Turned the ignition.

His car chuckled to life.

Lights blinked briefly on the dashboard.

The gentle rattle and hum of the engine trembled through the car.

He rested his hands on the steering wheel.

Although Goonherth Bay wasn't exactly teeming with local police keen to enforce drink-driving regulations he knew he would need to take it easy. He had lost count of the amount of drinks he'd had. Once he'd got to speaking with Henry Foldes his memory had simply run away with him. He had savoured recalling those countless resounding victories driven by Henry. It had been wonderful to recollect them with him. Having someone to throw memories around with was a sort of reassurance that he wasn't crazy. That what he believed to have happened in the past *had* actually happened.

Alexander reversed then headed for the road. As he trundled

between the school buildings, a pair of figures emerged from the murk.

Alexander brought the car to a halt.

As he tried to get a hold on his addled brain, he couldn't help the thought passing through his mind that these could be a pair of plain-clothes police officers. And that they had decided the Saint Camelgal High School reunion was the perfect opportunity for them to catch some drink drivers.

Already, Alexander's mind spiralled through the possibilities.

... *God*, it would be a pain!

He would lose his licence. He would be forced to cycle or get the bus every day.

And in the last year of his teaching career!

A series of wild fantasies flashed through his brain.

He thought about simply putting his foot down — rocketing away from the would-be police officers. Flying off into the night. He would swing through the narrow country lanes leading away from the school. Perhaps the police would call a helicopter to take part in the chase. And he would be forced to ditch the car, to bundle out into a ditch ...

Deciding he was allowing the drink to get to him more than it should, Alexander wound down the driver's window. The rain was still falling in a fine blanket.

These two people were getting wet.

One of them approached the driver's window while the other continued to block the path of Alexander's car.

"Anything the matter?" Alexander asked.

The person was wearing a transparent rain cape. A suit on beneath.

Finally, getting a good look at the face, Alexander recognised the individual.

Jock Jones.

The boy who had confronted him earlier today.

The one who had been a victim of that ... *incident* ...

"What ... what's going on?" Alexander asked, before adding dumbfoundedly, "I'm on my way home."

"Earlier," Jock said. "I wanted you to answer a question."

"A 'question'?" Alexander replied. "What ... what question?"

Jock didn't respond.

On instinct, Alexander glanced out front.

The figure who had blocked the exit of his car was gone.

Alexander wasn't going to stick around.

Instinctively he knew now was the time to get out of here.

As he brought up the clutch, ready to accelerate away, the car lurched forward into a stall. It was then that panic rippled through him. And then that he heard the passenger door open. He caught a final glance at Jock's face, still standing outside at his driver window, when he felt something firm — *sharp* — embed itself in his throat.

There was no pain. Only surprise. And then warmth.

As he felt himself going woozy, his mind drifting away, he heard Jock open the driver's door. Blackness clouded the periphery of his vision. He wasn't sure when he finally gave in. Only that he closed his eyes — just to rest them for a second ... and that was all it took for him to be swept away.

On the brink of his consciousness, he felt hands lifting him.

And some time later he heard the car engine rumble back into life.

When there was nothing — nothing but darkness — he knew it was the end.

ELENA

6.09 PM, SUNDAY

Inside the school hall, Elena was conscious of the head teacher Ghorsh striding purposefully toward the front of the stage. She knew, from the invitation she had seen only the day before, that the reunion was set to last until six pm.

And it had gone six.

The head teacher was rosy-cheeked and smiling as he raised his voice and addressed them. It wasn't until he had uttered his first few words that the hall descended into anything like silence.

"I would like to take this opportunity to thank you all for joining us today — it is always wonderful to see our former students; to have them *keep in touch*. And, for me, personally, it's fascinating to think of all of you who have passed through this very building and out into the wider world."

Elena shifted a glance about the crowd. Several people continued to speak among themselves. Some things never changed. Some people left school just as they arrived.

She looked back to the head teacher.

"Unfortunately," he continued, "all good things *must* come to an end. But I wish to thank you for coming and to wish you a safe journey home. I hope we'll meet again soon." With a smattering of applause, the head teacher descended the stage.

Headed for the exit, he stopped to shake a few hands on his way out. He struck Elena as having the air of a well-respected local politician.

The babble of the crowd started up again.

Elena blinked away her confusion. That was the problem with drinking in the middle of the day — it tended to disorient you. She turned her attention back to what was taking place around her. To the conversations — the hurried farewells.

It seemed strange this had all come to an end so promptly. Like they had stepped into a time warp ... but the world would soon be back to normal.

Day-to-day life would resume.

Elena thought about how she was going to get home.

She and Joanne had cycled here.

From the sound of the rain outside, returning home wasn't going to be an enviable prospect. Then again, she and Joanne had cycled in worse than drizzle. Once they had cycled together through snow — slipping and sliding through black ice and slush.

When Elena looked around for Joanne, her cycling buddy, she was in the company of Henry Foldes. As Elena took the two of them in, she couldn't help but think back to the meeting she had called the previous evening.

When they had spoken about "revenge".

Just what had she been thinking?

Just how *old* was she?

Of course, when she had called them all together, at her mother's house, she hadn't really had any plan in mind; other than ensuring Henry Foldes turned up to the reunion.

And yet, when she had seen Henry yesterday, she had been *consumed* by loathing — an urge to do *something*. Now, though, he seemed like a normal guy ... one of many.

So what if he had a "history"?

So *what* if he had a *dark* past?

Resigned to returning home alone, Elena made for the bike sheds.

Rain lashed down upon the playground asphalt.

Night draped over the school.

Only orange streetlights provided bursts of respite from the darkness.

She clutched her arms over her chest.

She hadn't dressed for adverse weather.

Feeling the chill of the rain running down the inside of her blouse, she reassured herself that the first thing she would do when she got home was take a hot shower.

And then everything would be fine.

She had just about got her bike off the rack, wrestled it free from the D-lock, when she heard voices approaching. She held still. Hidden in the shadows.

And listened.

Her stomach sank slightly when she sensed the voices coming closer.

God, she'd really had *enough* of the past ... she could just do with getting *away*.

She remained still as two people passed by.

Men.

She recognised one of the faces in profile.

Jock. Jock Jones.

He was speaking in a light, almost jubilant tone as they trudged their way back to the school building. She supposed the other person with him was Max.

A thrill ran through her heart. She had the sudden urge to call out. But something stopped her. Her voice failed her. She remained standing there with her bike.

Alone.

By the time Elena had wheeled her bike out towards the road, Jock and Max had already reached the school building. For some reason, she breathed a sigh of relief.

She realised she hadn't been looking forward to speaking with them.

They might have asked her to explain the next part of the "plan"

But there was *no* plan.

She threw her leg over the saddle and cycled off — turning onto the road.

Away from all this.

Away from the past.

JOCK
6.12 PM, SUNDAY

T he whole world was a blur.

  Everything had happened so quickly.

Everything had *played out* so neatly.

They had disposed of the body, and the car, in a nearby side-road.

Whenever Jock had tracked the real-life reports of murders on TV, he found himself constantly surprised by the idiocy of the killers.

How they never thought to do the obvious.

There had been no reason for them to run the car off a cliff ... or to roll it down into a ditch. It had been so simple to stow Mr Blindfield's body in the boot and park between dozens of other parallel-parked cars on the nearby street. Surely no one would uncover the car until it was reported lost, stolen. Or until Mr Blindfield was reported to have "gone missing". Jock planned to be long gone by the time *that* happened.

As they re-joined the reunion, they split up.

Jock took in the room, getting the impression that things were winding down. The day's frivolities coming to an inevitable end.

Thank *God.*

He really couldn't abide these gatherings.

Such an *idiocy*.

In his jacket pocket, Jock sensed the steady weight of the knife.

The flick knife he had taken from Max.

They had stopped by a stream on their way back to school and Jock had cleaned the blood from the knife, and his hands. The water had been freezing.

But these things needed to be done.

All the same, Jock couldn't help but check over his hands once again. It felt as if he was acting the role of Macbeth, paranoid someone would *somehow* be able to divine what he had done just from looking at him.

But his logical mind told him no one would suspect.

No one would suspect timid computer programmer, Jock Jones.

Jock wondered why he had returned at all when it was obvious that they would be turfed out in the course of the next fifteen minutes — that the overtime cleaners would be in here to clean things up before school resumed tomorrow.

It would hardly be appropriate for school children to remark on empty bottles of beer and champagne — spilled wine which lay in puddles beneath his feet.

Then it struck him why ... *why* he hadn't yet hopped in his car and driven home.

Now that he had killed he wanted another victim.

The one who he had fantasised about killing for ... *oh*, so long ...

He wanted to kill Henry Foldes.

As Elena had told them when she had invited them around to her house the previous night, this was all about *revenge*.

And revenge was what Jock was determined to have.

JOANNE

6.26 PM, SUNDAY

Joanne felt the mix of human heat and alcohol swilling about her brain.

The car was packed almost to bursting.

When she glanced over her shoulder, she saw no fewer than five had been squeezed into the back seat, while another couple had been rammed into the boot. Joanne herself was sitting on someone — *another woman's* — lap in the passenger seat. In fact, the only person travelling in any sort of comfort was the driver, Henry Foldes.

Harry.

She was still having trouble getting used to that.

Getting used to calling him by his name.

Though she was certain she'd catch onto the knack eventually.

As they barrelled their way up the hill, leading away from Saint Camelgal, Joanne caught a heady scent of something ... *nostalgia?* ... it was almost as if a part of her brain was telling her she would never return to the school again; as if she would leave Goonherth Bay behind and never come back. It was a weird fleeting feeling, but it stuck with her all the same. She took in Henry ... *Harry's* face in profile.

The wide smile spreading his cheeks.

It had of course taken her off guard when Harry — apparently spontaneously — had suggested they all go to The Crosses for the "after party". Although it might not have been the case, she believed herself to be the only one who fully understood the situation surrounding Harry's mother ... that she was dying ... that she was *close* to death.

But when she had given Harry a look, to question whether or not he was thinking straight, he had seemed to read her mind. He had held his lips close to her ear and whispered, "Mum always did enjoy a party."

Joanne hadn't believed it her place to judge.

And so, here they were now, in Harry's car, headed up the hill.

Headed for The Crosses.

When Joanne looked in the wing mirror, she saw three or four cars followed in their wake. She wondered dizzily if Harry had had the good grace to so much as *warn* his father of the forthcoming intrusion. But, then again, it wasn't really Joanne's business. She had no stake in this, after all.

Not really.

As Harry gripped the wheel — the car engine groaning and creaking and doing whatever else car engines do when they are reaching the limit of their operational capacity — Joanne noticed something ahead of them.

Moving through the gloom.

Her heart lurched up to her throat.

A chill ran through her bloodstream.

Her muscles stiffened.

It was all she could do to cry out, "*Stop!*" although Harry was ahead of her; jamming both feet down *hard* on the brakes.

The car halted suddenly.

From behind, Joanne heard the honking of horns and jubilant laughter.

No doubt they believed that some high-jinks had taken place here.

When Joanne turned her attention back front and centre, she realised she could no longer see the object which'd moved through the gloom.

It had vanished from view.

Melted into the darkness.

Finally, snapping to her senses, Joanne shucked out of the seat belt which pinned her, and the woman beneath her, to the passenger seat. With an awkward, fumbling struggle, she unlatched the door and tumbled out into the freezing-cold night air.

There was some more honking.

She resisted the urge to turn around.

She peered off into the darkness.

Saw nothing.

Joanne could hear someone stumbling out of the car behind her.

Someone called her name.

Still, she stayed facing forward.

It was nothing more than movement which caught the corner of her eye.

Off to the side of the road.

Something told her it was human.

A *human* motion.

After another few seconds her eyes grew accustomed to the darkness.

She made out the shape of a person emerging from the grassy verge.

Where they had tumbled over.

Slowly, they brought an object upright.

A bicycle.

At the time, if she'd given it thought, Joanne probably would've believed it to be the moonlight which allowed her to recognise Elena:

Her best friend.

However, the truth most likely was that they'd spent so much time together that Joanne had learned to recognise Elena above and beyond her mere facial features.

"El?" Joanne said, unable to keep the surprise out of her voice.

Elena blinked slowly, clearly startled at the sudden tumble off her bike.

The spokes of the front wheel had buckled.

"Are you hurt?" Joanne asked.

Elena looked over herself, rubbed at her forearm. "Just a few scrapes, I think. That's all." She took a step forward, winced. "And my left leg doesn't feel great."

"Nothing broken, though?"

"I don't think so."

"I didn't realise you'd left," Joanne said.

"No," Elena replied before adding as if it was necessary, "I was ... I was just going *home*."

"When I looked about for you ... I couldn't find you."

Elena looked beyond Joanne, to the car.

Joanne might've been wrong but she thought she appeared slightly dazed.

"Looks like you've got a party planned," Elena said. "Henry's house?"

A silence opened up before them.

And Joanne knew she had to ask the question.

"Do you ... want to come?" Joanne asked.

Leaning over her bike, Elena glanced over Joanne's shoulder, to the car, as if making certain this wasn't some mirage. "Are there ... are there two people sitting in the boot?"

"There's probably room for *three* at a squeeze."

"Doesn't look like you've got room for a bike, though."

Joanne gave a slight smile. "I left mine at school." She glanced back to the cars following Harry's. She jerked her thumb in their direction. "I'm sure someone can fit a bike in one of those. It doesn't look like you're going to be riding it any time soon."

If Joanne had been able to properly make out Elena's expression, she supposed it would've communicated the quagmire of the time warp they found themselves sucked down into. Not unlike how Joanne was feeling herself right now.

"I should be getting home," Elena said finally.

"So should I."

Elena considered for another few seconds before making up her mind. "Okay," she replied. "I'll come. Just for a little while."

"Great," Joanne replied. "That's great."

HENRY

6.39 PM, SUNDAY

H arry heard them in the drawing room.
That was where he had led them.

That was where the *booze* was located.

He fumbled through the cabinets in the kitchen, searching for anything which might improve the party — snacks, extra glasses.

What was he *doing*?

His mother was upstairs.

She was *dying*.

This might well be her last night on Earth ... and he was here ... with a bunch of people he had ceased to think about until ... this afternoon.

Until tonight.

The truth was that over the course of the past few hours his mind had become consumed with the idea of Joanne Darkly. He had no idea what sort of trick she had played on him; whether or not she might've *hypnotised* him somehow.

Great ... now he was starting to sound like his father.

Harry dug out a handful of glasses, some packets of what he

hoped would be *in date* crisps, and dumped them on the counter. He heard footsteps over his shoulder.

He prepared himself for his beleaguered father, searching for an explanation for the sudden appearance of all these people. However, when Harry turned, he saw it was Jasmine. She must've been in one of the cars which'd followed him here.

He took in her blond hair and whip-smart eyes, seeming to judge anything and everything in a fell swoop. Jasmine — his *ex*-girlfriend Jasmine.

To tell the truth, Harry would've much rather had her *not* be here but when he had announced this impromptu "after party" it had seemed impractical — if not inappropriate — to single people out for exclusion. The others surely saw it as a rehash of one of his famous school-era house parties. When, all the time, the only reason he had ever thrown those parties — invited people over — was in the hope that he might get close to Joanne Darkly. And last night he finally had.

Tonight the motivation had been no different from those house parties in his past.

He was worried — *terrified even* — that he might lose Joanne.

That they might never see one another again.

For several moments, Harry was rendered stunned by the sight of Jasmine before him. She seemed to stand centre stage within his mind. He tried to make sense of her.

He tried to work out what she *meant*.

She took a few steps toward him, her mouth turning at the corners in a smile.

"You have *no idea* how long I've been waiting," she said.

Before Harry had the chance to react — the chance to defend himself — Jasmine threw her arms about his neck. She tugged his mouth down onto hers. And, before Harry could do anything, they were kissing.

The kiss might've lasted for a minute or more before he felt her fingertips tracing the crotch of his trousers. He tried to resist, but, well, he was *still* that oversexed schoolboy he had always been. The one who people had always told *tales* about.

As she worked her fingers past the waistband of his trousers, she spoke softly in his ear. "You know," she said, "I always *did* want to know a little more about your history than you would tell me."

She squeezed his penis so hard that it hurt.

Harry flinched.

Felt her fingernails press into the soft sensitive skin.

"Joanne," she said, her voice icy cool. "Did you ... you know ... *ever?*"

Jasmine's hold on his penis squeezed tighter still.

The sensation shifted from discomfort to out-and-out pain.

He glanced about as if he needed someone to help him. As if he needed someone to help him with *Jasmine* ... the woman had the physique of a frustrated model, for Chrissake. He had to get it together.

He looked her in the eye.

Felt the burn just beneath the surface.

His thoughts turned to the question which Jasmine had asked.

And his mind inevitably twirled back to the previous night.

To the night he and Joanne had spent together.

Harry made the effort to speak. "I ... don't think it's really ... your ... *business.*"

It seemed that, with each one of his words, she twisted her grip more tightly.

He was concerned she might venture further south.

Focus her attention on his testicles.

There was only so much pain a man could take.

Jasmine continued to glare, and then, as if someone had flipped a switch in her brain, she broke off her stare. As if remembering herself — *realising* they weren't a pair of confused sex-crazed teenagers any longer — she released her hold.

Feeling tender, Harry backed away, concerned about a follow-up attack.

Jasmine strutted about the kitchen in a feline fashion, as if the house belonged to her. He supposed that, judging from the time she had spent here, throughout her youth, she might remember The Crosses as some sort of "second home".

Well, perception was one thing, and reality was quite another.

Harry flirted with the idea of asking her to leave ... but he couldn't help thinking that was an *exceptionally* bad one. There was a high risk of "setting her off".

No, it was better to play it cool.

He could make sure someone got her good and drunk.

That was always an effective method of taking care of troublesome cases. They couldn't cause so much trouble when they were struggling to see straight.

Or when they had to stumble to the toilet every fifteen minutes.

With this thought on his mind, Harry checked through the kitchen cabinets.

He uncovered a couple of bottles:

Brandy and rum.

His mother and father used them for cooking.

He handed the bottles to Jasmine.

She took them from him, with a smile.

Harry forced himself to grin in response. "To get the party started."

"Oh-kay," Jasmine replied.

As she took the bottles, she leaned in and planted a heavy kiss on his lips.

In that moment, Harry found himself whipped back at lightning speed; to a time which he had believed to be long past. All those moments he thought he'd long forgotten. Wild, hot, *sweaty*, passionate nights together.

Harry had never been *in love* with Jasmine — he'd never been *in love* with anyone.

But he thought of her fondly.

Not that he would ever say so much out loud.

Bottles in hand, Jasmine picked her way across the kitchen. She paused in the doorway, clutching the bottles to her chest. She puckered her lips, blew a kiss, *winked*.

When she'd gone, Harry allowed himself a moment, looking out the window, over the darkened garden, to the bay beyond. He wondered if people even lived in the real world at all. How had he found himself here?

On this planet?

In this universe?

Were humans really anything other than the seemingly random thoughts and urges whizzing through their minds?

ELENA
6.45 PM, SUNDAY

E lena glanced about the drawing room.

She recognised the faces — all of them, without exception — even though they were *warped* by laughter. It was almost as if she had stepped into some art exhibition inside her own mind; a sort of *interpretation* of her own thoughts and memories all laid out for her perusal. When her eyes fell on Joanne, conversing with Adam Glee-tarth — one of those who Mr Blindfield had namechecked in his speech back at school ... one of those who he *clearly* remembered fondly.

Elena approached Joanne who currently bore a tumbler of whisky in her hand.

Elena stood on the periphery of the conversation until she judged there was a suitable pause. When it came around, she took hold of Joanne's hand and led her out of the drawing room and into the corridor. They walked together some way until they came across the music room.

In the doorway, Elena hesitated wondering if she should venture in.

This *was* a house party after all and whenever Henry had put on parties in his youth there had never been "boundaries" ... nothing to get in the way of the *fun.*

Elena scanned the framed photographs which hung on the walls, all of the concerts which Henry's father had played. Then she cast her gaze onto the grand piano which occupied a good proportion of the room. Finally, her eyes slipped beyond, identifying a nook over by the window which looked out on the garden, and on Goonherth Bay.

Thinking it was for the best, Elena drew the doors shut behind them.

They needed *a little* privacy.

Elena needed a little privacy.

Once Elena had Joanne sat down on the pillows on the window ledge, she felt she had achieved some sort of intimacy. It felt as if the two of them were *truly* alone now.

She stared into Joanne's eyes, hoping to attain some level of sincerity ... doing her best to divorce this moment from the *light-hearted* tone which'd accompanied the rest of the reunion. "I've noticed you and Henry getting ... close."

Joanne's features darkened.

"Look," Elena said, "this won't take long. I promise. There's something you need to know. Something you need to know if you ... if you *plan* on becoming more involved."

Elena waited for an interruption, but Joanne seemed happy to hear her out.

It was best for her just to ... *show* Joanne what she was dealing with ...

Elena rose.

She peeled down the waistband of her trousers.

Showing off her underwear, Elena felt suddenly self-conscious.

On instinct, she glanced up to the doorway.

There was no one there.

There was no reason for her to fear.

It was just her and Joanne — Joanne and *her.*

Elena brought her trousers down to just above her knees,

exposing her upper thighs. And her underwear, too, of course. She had gone with a no-frills white thong that particular day. No "granny" pants to be embarrassed about.

Joanne looked bemused.

Perhaps due to the low illumination in the room — only moonlight seeped in — Joanne had trouble discerning what Elena was showing her.

In the end, though, Joanne saw.

She *definitely* saw.

Her hands rushed for her mouth in a cartoonish gasp.

Elena remained standing for another few seconds, allowing Joanne to fully appreciate the sight which confronted her; to fully grasp the implications.

When Elena brought her trousers back up over her waistline, she noted how Joanne remained fixated on the spot. As if she was able to see through the fabric.

"He did it," Elena said.

" 'He' ?"

"Henry. *Harry.*"

Joanne sat very still.

Her eyes finally left the spot on Elena's inner thigh.

She glanced briefly at Elena's face and then turned her attention out of the window, out across the garden. In a muffled voice, almost to herself, she said, "I'd heard stories ... I'd ..."

Elena waited for Joanne to say something further.

But she said *nothing*.

Silence pressed down on both of them.

Elena thought she could almost feel the silence itself *prickling* her skin. "Do you want to go home?" Elena asked.

Joanne remained where she was, staring out the window, looking across the still waters of the bay as drizzle blanketed the landscape. "... No," she finally replied. Reaching out for Elena, touching her tenderly on the forearm as if silently acknowledging the fortitude it'd taken Elena to show her, she added, "But I want to stay here for a while. With you." A faint smile crept across her lips.

Elena smiled back.

But it was an empty smile.

Her heart felt like a pebble dangling from a string, rebounding off her ribs.

She had told Joanne something deeply personal.

And Joanne had held back.

Perhaps they weren't "best friends" after all.

JOCK

6.56 PM, SUNDAY

Jock pulled up to a halt alongside the other cars parked outside The Crosses.

On the way here, he had toyed with the idea of just turning around, of skipping town. But in the end he had decided this was something he just had to do.

He had to finish what he had started.

Henry Foldes was his own personal battle.

A battle which was reaching its end stages.

Once Jock had switched off the ignition, and had taken in the well-lit facade of The Crosses, he began to have second thoughts.

He hadn't been invited.

Back at school, he and Henry had never been friends, of course, and yet Jock had still felt as though he knew him. Popular students always lived their lives out in public.

And just like everyone else he had heard the rumours.

The voluptuous house parties with no rules ... or *almost* no rules.

How would the party tonight compare to those?

Everyone was more mature.

Everyone had grown into their adult lives.

Others had never had a chance.

That chance had been taken away from them.

If only Jock had been given the *same* chance as everyone else.

But Henry Foldes had denied him.

Still gripping the steering wheel with one hand, he reached into his jacket pocket and withdrew the flick knife. He flipped the blade open.

Stared along the edge.

Held it up to the light emanating from the house.

The knife seemed an almost divine object.

Like it held godlike properties.

He supposed it *did* possess godlike properties.

It held the power to take life away.

He drew a profound breath, felt it puff up his lungs, stretch his stomach muscles.

His whole body seemed prepared.

Ready for action.

Did athletes feel this way before a big game?

Before a big performance?

When Jock glanced up again at the house, a tremor passed through his bones.

Now.

Now was the time.

Before he lost his nerve.

STEPHEN
6.58 PM, SUNDAY

As Stephen Foldes prowled the upper floors of The Crosses, he realised he could hear voices downstairs.

Visitors.

His son had company.

That was all right with him, of course. If it hadn't been for his son's antics, back when he'd been younger, then Stephen supposed he never would've had any contact with the outside world. It had been his decision, to seal themselves off, in the countryside. *Far* away from everyone, and everything.

It was for the best.

The only way he could control himself.

... And his *issues* of being around other people.

Stephen rested his hands on the banister and looked down the staircase.

His mind felt stretched.

That was what liquor and a lack of sleep did.

He glanced back over his shoulder and considered whether he should return to his wife's bedside. He wondered how many hours he had spent in her company. He seemed to have been forever waiting for her to wake up, for her to sit up.

To get "better".

It was probably just the solitude getting to him.

All of the time spent alone.

All of the *silence*.

In actual fact, it was good to hear the *babble* of the relatively young about the house again. It sent a fresh jig through his heart.

Made him feel alive again.

Stephen drew breath, closed his eyes tight and bowed his head over the banister.

What could he do now?

He was dimly aware of the doorbell chiming in the front hall.

It jerked him from his daze.

Brought him back to reality with a thud.

He stepped back from the banister and allowed the dressing gown draped around his shoulders to drop at his feet. He trod his way to the bedroom.

And his wardrobe.

JASMINE

6.59 PM, SUNDAY

Hearing the doorbell chime, Jasmine rose up out of the armchair. She stumbled a few steps, catching herself against the dining room wall. She shook her head.

It was strange.

She'd lost count of the drinks she had knocked back during the day.

As if she'd been drinking nothing but water.

Jasmine unlatched the door, bringing the cold, damp night air into the dry, roasting warmth of The Crosses. She squinted at the person on the doorstep.

A *vague* recollection ...

Perhaps it was the long hair.

Or maybe something more subtle.

In the end, though, the net result was the same.

The name popped into her mind:

Jock. Jock *Jones*.

There were good reasons for her to recall Jock Jones beyond his mere name and appearance. He had been one of Henry's ... *victims*.

Jock stared out at her.

She gave the suit he wore a once-over. She had to admit she was surprised he had a *semblance* of how to dress. That was more than could be said for most men. Then again, it could just as easily be explained away by a doting wife, or fashion consultant ...

Because she saw no reason to deny him entry, Jasmine stepped to one side.

As Jock passed through the doorway, she couldn't help noticing the earthy scent which clung to him. She also noted his drawn-out features ... how his eyeballs were sunken in their sockets. She supposed she didn't look all that great either given that she'd been drinking all day.

"What do I see before me? A *ghost?*" Jasmine said, with a mock aristocratic voice.

She realised listening to her own voice that she was further gone than she'd expected.

To her surprise, Jock managed a smile.

And it wasn't even a *creepy* smile.

Was it just her imagination or had Jock really ... *grown into himself?*

As she stood there, half leaning up against the wall, regarding him, she couldn't help but acknowledge the plan hatching in her mind; one which in her drunken state seemed somewhat divine. She tilted her head to one side. "You ... used to be ... *fatter.*"

Jock's smile widened. "Not particularly," he replied. "They always used to call me 'lanky streak of piss'."

Jasmine realised her memory was muddled.

She was confusing Jock with someone else.

Another of Henry's victims.

A *fat* one.

She pressed on a smile, told herself to take this in her stride.

Nobody's memory was *perfect.*

She watched him closely, in a catlike fashion, as he brought the door shut behind him. She held her hands clasped behind her back, and lightly bounced off the wall. "And what brings you here, Jock Jones?"

"I wanted to join the party."

Jasmine was taken aback by his sure, confident tone.

She was used to her forthright manner knocking men off their stride. It was a quality she was proud of and one which she'd held since she'd been a school girl.

"Well," she replied, with a smile, "You've certainly come to the right place." It was here that she decided to make her move. That if she planned — if she *really* planned — to win Henry Foldes back then there was no time like the present.

She gently pushed herself away from the wall.

For some reason, it seemed like a good idea to make a *whoosh* sound.

In her mind's eye she imagined herself as a rocket.

Blasting up to space.

She took a step forward, feeling for the edge of a loose floorboard.

She pushed onto her other foot, toppling into Jock.

As she had hoped, he caught hold of her.

Kept her from falling flat on her face.

There was no mistaking his steady grip.

Or the bulging muscles.

She was sure he could overwhelm her physically if he really wanted to.

"*Splat!*" she cried out with a hyper giggle.

Jock, too, seemed to find this humorous.

She was glad.

As he cradled her in his arms, she looked into his eyes.

Lost herself for a moment.

There was something ... *some* ... *thing* ...

Was it sadness? Some *secret*?

With these thoughts fixed in her mind she felt herself melting into him.

Pressing her lips up against his.

The whole world spun around.

JOANNE

7.05 PM, SUNDAY

T he silhouette standing at the double doors to the music room
startled Joanne.

She rose from her seat.

Elena stood too.

Joanne watched the doors open. She recognised the figure.

It was Harry's father:

Stephen Foldes.

It was slightly eerie to have all those Stephen Foldeses — as
depicted in the framed concert posters hanging on the wall — staring
down at them while having the real thing standing before her.
Although he wasn't an especially impressive man stature-wise it was
undeniable that there *was* something about him.

It was what the critics termed "presence".

He knew how to stand.

How to *allow* himself to be admired.

He certainly seemed dressed for the occasion.

He wore a finely pressed tuxedo with a jet-black cummerbund.
The suit material glistened in the moonlight which leaked in. "Bit
dark in here, don't you think?" he said.

He flipped a light switch.

Warm orange lights flickered on about the room.

Even though Joanne had heard Stephen Foldes on many different occasions, she couldn't help but think about how his raw, street-styled Cockney accent clashed with the image he projected to the world.

This man of high art.

A genius of his generation.

It seemed almost like a bastardisation of his purpose; a way of bringing down to earth that which should've been the property of the clouds.

Stephen Foldes stepped into the room, holding his shoulders rigid. Although Joanne had seen him last the night before, she couldn't help but note just how well he had managed to hold his figure. His stomach still seemed flat — unburdened by a beer gut. Since the Foldeses were notorious for not leaving The Crosses, she couldn't help but wonder what his secret might be:

Did he exercise?

Some dietary secret?

Now was hardly the time to ask.

Remembering herself, the situation, Joanne said, "How is your wife, Mr Foldes?"

"*Stephen*, please," he replied, and then pressed on a firmer smile still. "She is upstairs — in bed ... she needs her rest ..."

Joanne thought he might add something else, but he remained quiet.

Feeling that she needed to fill the silence to prevent it becoming overwhelming, Joanne said, "Henry invited us here. If it's a problem, we'll be only too pleased to leave. You just need to say the word, of course, and we — "

But he hushed her with a single swift gesture.

A flap of his hand.

Joanne couldn't help imagining the countless orchestras which must've been silenced by that same gesture.

He gestured to himself. "Do I *look* dressed as if I came to tell you all to go home?"

Joanne took in his tuxedo again.

Thought through his question.

"No," she replied. "No, you don't."

"Well, then," he said.

He approached Elena.

Smiled.

"And you, my dear," he said, holding out his hand. "I don't *believe* I've ever had the pleasure."

"El ... Elena," she replied, allowing him to take her hand in his.

Stephen stooped to kiss the back of her hand.

As he straightened up, he muttered, "Surname?"

"Kardos."

He cocked his head to one side.

Pursed his lips.

"*Hungarian?*"

Elena slipped Joanne a glance.

Joanne wasn't sure how to interpret it.

"That's right," Elena replied. "My mother is from Hungary."

"I could hear it in your tone of *voice*. The way you *crush* your consonants ..." He flashed an impossibly charming smile. "And your surname, of course." He clasped his chin in his fingers. Seemed to stare at a point in mid-air. "A child," he said. "Young. About ..." He snapped his fingers. "Less than a year old?"

Joanne found herself switching from Stephen to Elena.

Elena's complexion had gone quite pale.

"That's right," Elena replied.

"And the child's name ... let me guess ... a regal name, is it?"

"I suppose so."

"G, G, G, G ..."

Joanne caught the panicked glance from Elena, though what Elena precisely wanted escaped Joanne completely.

Finally, Stephen settled on the name of Elena's child. "... *George*," he said. "That's his name, isn't it?"

Elena was rendered dumbstruck.

Finally, she replied, in a croaky voice, "Yes."

A silence settled over the room.

Joanne felt an unpleasant prickling sensation pass over the surface of her skin. She felt the blood pumping up to her skull. A chill ran right through her bones, down to the very tips of her toes.

"Mr Foldes ... *Stephen*," Joanne said, correcting herself.

"Yes?"

"Would you, uh, mind playing us *something*?"

As if clarification were required, she nodded in the direction of the grand piano.

Stephen furrowed his brow, losing his easy smile for the first time.

Joanne scolded herself for saying anything at all. She had said what she said because she felt uncomfortable with the quietness, with the formal tone which'd descended upon them.

But now she realised her error.

Stephen Foldes *never* played the piano.

He hadn't in years.

In *decades*, even.

And yet, there was the grand piano, ivory keys bare, *begging* to be played.

And he was dressed to give a concert ...

Joanne thought it a sin that a genius like Stephen no longer indulged his gift.

His *talent*.

Not that it had anything to do with her ...

Stephen eyed Joanne very closely, and then, right when she was certain he would leap into some blazing rage, that he would demand that they *Get out, get out!*, he became very calm. He smiled lightly. And then, in a reverent manner, he bowed his head.

Ventured over to the piano.

And took his seat at the stool.

HENRY

7.13 PM, SUNDAY

To begin with, Harry could hardly believe his ears.

The sound of the grand piano drifting through the corridors.

Mournful notes plucked with precise detail.

It was almost like a wave ... washing in over him.

When he looked up from where he sat slouched in an armchair, in the corner of the drawing room, he crossed eyes with Edward Wanton.

Edward had been so faithful to him when they had been young ...

It was strange Harry was so loath to define him as a "friend" now.

That definition implied too much by the way of *equality* and if either of them were honest about their relationship then there was very little that was equal about it.

Harry had given the orders.

Always.

Edward's eyes nearly bulged from their sockets as he perched on the edge of the sofa, rocking back and forth gently. Harry wondered what he might have taken.

What *habits* he might've acquired throughout the years.

It was a long time since they'd been relatively innocent young men.

Harry turned his attention to the tumbler of whisky he clutched in his fist, his elbow resting on the arm of his chair. He took in the amber colour of the whisky, sparkling slightly in the warmly lit haze of the drawing room. He wondered how much he had had to drink. He supposed he had lost count after the first couple.

This couldn't be his third, could it?

As Harry lazily took stock of the drawing room, the near-maniacal laughter which echoed off the walls, he thought about how his mother was upstairs ... *dying*.

This had been his idea.

He had invited these people.

He had wanted to hear laughter one more time in this house before he left forever.

He supposed he had also wanted to recapture. That he had wanted to *absorb* all that had happened to him in his childhood. And then lock it away in a cupboard.

The piano music worked on Harry like a massage, pummelling him deeper into the armchair. Causing him to *sink* into the cushions. An irrational fear blurred through his mind. That he might sink all the way into the armchair.

And choke to death.

Harry rocked himself onto his feet. He staggered from side to side, finding balance. He narrowed his eyes, attempting to bring the room a little sharper.

Attempting to stop the edges blurring so much.

He looked Edward in the eye, nodded to him and then left the room.

Whether or not Edward noticed him, Harry couldn't tell and didn't really care.

Once out in the corridor, hearing that smooth, tragic music washing over him, Harry felt his bottom lip wobble. His whole body seemed to struggle with the sound. It had been a long time ... *much* longer than he could remember ... when his father had last played the piano.

Not since *that* night.

Harry took several deep breaths. He gripped the tumbler of whisky to his chest.

He gazed up the staircase to his mother and father's room ... to where he knew his mother would be lying upon her bed awaiting *death*.

He couldn't help but smile wanly.

This was so ridiculous ... this *whole* situation was so ridiculous ...

And yet it *was* happening to him.

Harry rested his head against the wall of the hallway.

It felt as if invisible hands were kneading his brain.

It wasn't fair ... *none* of this was fair.

While he lurked in the shadows, he realised he could hear giddy laughter.

A familiar laugh.

When he turned to look, he saw a couple emerging from the drawing room.

It took him only a moment to recognise the first face:

Jasmine.

As drunk as she had been back in the kitchen.

Her features were all creased — *distorted*.

As always, she was the one taking the lead.

Unseen in the shadows, Harry watched as Jasmine led the man with her onward.

It took him a moment to recognise the second face.

But he managed in the end.

Jock.

Jock *Jones*.

The one who had suffered that "unfortunate" accident in the changing rooms.

He eyed how Jock Jones had transformed into a man now, and how his long, black hair hung freely between his shoulder blades.

Harry observed Jasmine drunkenly leading the seemingly reluctant Jock up the staircase. Both of them were smiling, but whereas Jasmine's expression was one of reckless abandon, Jock's was more a nervous grin ... clearly concerned about them being discovered. Harry could just imagine the sort of thrill which might be passing through Jock to believe that he was about to bed Henry Foldes's "childhood sweetheart".

And in his own *home*!

Wouldn't it be such great payback for what Harry had done?

As they disappeared from sight, at the top of the stairs, Harry couldn't help but smirk. He wondered if Jock was even still a man. If he could even still *perform*.

Perhaps Jasmine was just as curious to know the answer.

Or perhaps she was somehow oblivious.

In the near distance, Harry heard the piano music descend into nothing.

Into silence.

His vision cleared.

His mind felt lucid now.

The world somehow *brighter*.

When he headed for the music room, he walked with a steady gait.

He was back in control.

JASMINE

7.18 PM, SUNDAY

The pitch blackness upstairs was unbearable.

It pressed into Jasmine on all sides.

What was she doing?

Her heart throbbed in her throat.

She felt strange ... nervous?

But she had to follow this through.

It was the only way to get to Harry.

The only way to *really* get to him.

She squeezed Jock's hand tighter.

Casually sank her fingernails into the fleshy part of his palm.

This was all part of her strategy. She knew the effect it had on men. It brought blood to the surface. It stopped them thinking clearly.

Almost like witchcraft.

Jasmine envisioned the scene. How afterwards she would descend the staircase, arm in arm with Jock, both wearing contented smiles. In her fantasy, she imagined Harry standing on the bottom step, a look of confusion ... *hurt* sketched across his face.

Maybe then he would understand what it was like to be in her shoes.

Although it had been decades since Jasmine had last visited The Crosses, it wasn't difficult to locate one of the many guest bedrooms. When she pushed back the first door, she was taken aback to see white dust covers draped over the furniture within.

There was something eerie and sad about the abandoned room.

Unperturbed, she backed out, drawing Jock closer.

She had more luck with the next door.

Jasmine slammed the door shut behind them, smashing the light switch as she went. As the crystal chandelier came alive with warm orange light, she couldn't stop the memories flooding her mind. One rainy Sunday she and Harry had made a game of rushing between every room of The Crosses and making love in each and every one. By the end, Jasmine recalled how worn out she had been.

The next day at school had passed in a contented daze.

She flushed the recollections from her mind.

That was the past.

And this was her present.

Jock Jones.

He was still wearing his jacket.

Reaching up, staring into his dilated, wondering pupils, she slipped her fingers in beneath his collar, gently easing his jacket down his arms. She allowed it to tumble to their feet with a satisfying, louder-than-expected, *thump*.

Eyes still fixated on his, she grabbed his hand and dragged him stumbling towards the made-up bed. They got about halfway when Jock jerked her to a stop.

Bemused and trying not to show that she was put out by this temporary show of resistance, Jasmine said, "What's the matter, honey?"

"Can we switch off the lights?" he asked.

She analysed the request.

Wondered how she felt about it.

A question normally more typical of a woman ... which was to say that it was within *her* power as a woman to ask. Not his, as a man.

She could stop this right now if she wanted.

She relinquished his hand.

"Why?"

"I'd feel more comfortable."

"Got someone else on your mind?"

Jock's lips remained pressed together.

Expression neutral.

Jasmine was on the brink of storming out but she held herself back. That was how she might've acted as a teenager ... but now she was a full-grown woman.

She reminded herself of her plan.

Of Harry.

In a way it was fair.

Because she was thinking of someone else too.

She picked her way past Jock and slapped the lights off with the heel of her palm, instantly killing the illumination from the chandelier above.

It was only as her eyes became accustomed to the darkness that Jasmine realised there was a full moon tonight. A slice of its milky ray cut through the gap in the curtains.

With a single swift motion, she threw open the curtains.

Moonlight pooled into the room.

Setting the two of them in its half light.

There was something ... *ethereal* about the encounter now.

Jasmine was caught by a sobering moment.

She wondered what she was doing.

What *was* she doing?

She looked Jock over again.

And remembered.

As she worked to strip him of his shirt and dress trousers, Jasmine waited for him to reciprocate. Or even take the lead.

But he simply stood still and watched.

Before long, she had him stripped down to his underwear.

A pair of white briefs.

Now she hesitated.

She peered up into Jock's eyes.

An empty stare.

She eased her fingertips in around the waistband of his underwear.

Drew back the elastic.

Gently she drew his pants down.

Over his thighs.

And then past his kneecaps.

When she reached his ankles, she paused, waiting for him to diligently lift his feet.

One after the other.

Naked.

Now he was *naked*.

It was almost as if Jasmine had sculpted a statue out of marble.

She stood back to admire her handiwork.

And this time she couldn't prevent her eyes from venturing downward.

From venturing *south* of his belly button.

Perhaps she had imagined she would see nothing but a vacant space.

Smooth skin.

A *eunuch*.

However, even in the eerie half-light, she could make out the phallic form.

It was limp.

"Without life", she might've said, in crueller moments.

Jock was staring off at some point in mid-air.

He reminded her of a soldier standing on parade — awaiting inspection.

"Can I ... ?" Jasmine began.

She didn't complete the question and Jock said nothing in reply.

Jasmine took the non-response as affirmation.

She drew a deep breath and reached for his penis.

She felt the supple, slick, leathery skin.

Her fingers gradually moved further downward and she felt for Jock's testicles.

But there was nothing but scarred tissue.

A tremble passed through her.

Her heart hammered her tongue.

She was afraid to look Jock in the eye.

"What ..." she began. "How ... ?"

"Henry," Jock replied, as if the answer was obvious.

Jasmine wasn't entirely certain if it was shock or repulsion.

Or a combination of both.

When Jock spoke again his voice was so abrupt and loud that it made her flinch.

As if he had physically struck her.

"Lie down."

Although Jasmine had never imagined herself to be the type of woman who would do something just because a man said so, this time it was different.

She retreated from him.

It felt as if she was hypnotised by a spell binding them together.

She trod backwards, towards the bed.

It was only when she was lying down, gradually peeling off her own clothes, that she realised the power in the room had shifted. She was no longer in control.

She had surrendered control to Jock.

How it had happened ... she couldn't say.

Jock was crouching down now, fishing through the jacket she had shoved free of his shoulders.

A cloud drifted across the sky outside and the room was plunged into darkness.

Her breathing came shallower.

And her heart beat faster still.

More than anything she wanted to escape.

She wanted to *back out* of this encounter.

And yet she knew there would be no escape.

Not now.

She had to go through with what she had started.

Jock held his arms down at his sides as he approached.

Jasmine's attention was fixed on his penis.

She thought she saw some life.

She *believed* she saw it twitch.

Stiffen slightly.

A slight warmth entered her blood — that female sense of accomplishment.

That *she* had done that.

But almost as soon as the sense of accomplishment had dawned, it departed.

Replaced by coldness.

Replaced by fear.

Jock lay down, rolled onto his side so he faced into her.

She felt his body warmth. But it was no comfort from the chill.

Jasmine was halfway to rising up, to making some excuse to liberate herself from Jock's company, when she felt his insistent touch just beneath her breasts.

Urging her down.

Flat onto her back.

She acquiesced.

As she lay there, staring through the darkness, up at the ceiling, she felt Jock's tongue exploring her body.

Finding her nipples.

And then venturing further downward — beneath her waistline.

It sent cold skitters through her.

And then she felt his hardness.

It was at that point when everything changed utterly.

When the thrill passed through her chest.

She reached for his head — for that *long* hair of his.

Gave it a playful tug.

Jock grunted.

Jasmine smiled to herself.

She had been hasty to judge.

She still had control.

She was still in charge.

She had more power than she could ever imagine.

She only had to exercise it.

The hardness made its way up her thigh — slowly advancing.

She waited for Jock to spread his weight over her, to find his place between her legs. When he did, she allowed her head to sink back into the pillow.

And closed her eyes.

Thought of Harry.

The hardness carried on its way — up her body.

Soon it was at her stomach.

And then her breasts.

Finally, it settled at her throat.

She felt its steady weight there.

A sort of ... *what?*

Sharpness!

As the thought passed through her mind, Jasmine suddenly felt the warmth in her throat — the thick, suffocating gooey sensation.

She couldn't breathe.

A bitter copperlike scent pierced the air.

It twirled up her nostrils.

When she tried to scream, she couldn't.

There was simply no air in her lungs.

Her strength was rapidly deserting her.

It was through half-closed eyelids that she took in Jock's form in the darkness.

Moonlight shimmered across the blade.

Where had the knife come from?
The jacket?
Already the questions began to fade into the back of her mind ...
Darkness seeped into the corners of her vision.
And soon there was nothing.

ELENA
7.24 PM, SUNDAY

The rain had let off when Elena stepped outside.

She trod over to the stone statue.

She took in the form of the cherubic boy. One of his hands formed a fist and pressed into his hip. There was a loincloth wrapped about his waist. She followed the boy's gaze. He looked off across the garden, in the direction of Goonherth Bay.

She wondered if the statue had been here when the Foldeses had moved in or if Henry's father Stephen had acquired it, deciding it would make an excellent decoration.

Something about the statue was greatly weird.

There was something deeply disconcerting about the boy.

It put her in mind of an apparition.

If she'd woken in the middle of the night and looked out of one of the windows she might've mistaken the statue for a phantom. Then again, when it came to things that went bump in the dark she had always had a low threshold.

"Thought I might find you out here."

Elena startled, turned.

She looked to the door which led back into the house.

And the person standing there.

None other than Henry Foldes.

All of a sudden, his expression changed from gleeful surprise to genuine shock.

"Oh," he said, "I thought that you were ... never mind."

Elena knew he had believed she was Joanne.

There could be no other explanation.

It was conceivable, of course, that he might've mistaken her for Jasmine — that Henry might've thought that Elena was his childhood lover — but Elena had seen the expression which'd crossed his face. How his expression had been twisted into something Elena was only able to describe as *ecstasy*.

Elena could spot True Love at fifty paces.

And it *had* been True Love ... at least for Henry.

Elena half expected Henry to apologise and venture back into the house.

But he didn't.

He stood his ground and then he trod the gravel which surrounded the statue.

He gave the statue a quick once-over and then bowed his head.

Elena noted the tumbler of whisky dangling from his hand.

Was Henry an alcoholic?

Was that who he had grown up to be?

Or was this just a night of merriment?

"I think," Henry began, pacing around the statue, peering down, "that an apology might be in order."

"An 'apology' ?" Elena replied, surprised. Catching a second wind, realising the alcohol might be numbing Henry's senses, she said, "You already apologised."

Henry glanced up momentarily. He gave her the faintest of smiles before furrowing his brow and returning his focus to the glass in his hand. "I ... mean about what happened. What happened between us." He paused then added, "A long time ago."

Elena's chest tightened.

It felt as if every muscle seized up.

It was a wonder she didn't topple over.

Feeling a fresh breeze blowing in, she folded her arms over her chest. There was no use in pretending she didn't know exactly what he was talking about.

They both knew perfectly well.

When she caught a glimpse of Henry's face, she realised he was crying.

Tears running down his cheeks.

Elena felt a fury sweep through her.

He had no reason to be upset.

She had all the reason to be upset.

All the same, she couldn't completely suppress the urge to comfort him.

No matter who it was, she always wanted to Make Things Better.

"You have to understand," Henry said, still pacing the circumference of the statue, "that I was a different *person* then."

He halted his advance.

Peered down into his glass.

Next, he drew back his arm and tossed the glass off into the darkness.

Elena heard the *tinkle* of crystal breaking in the distance.

She wondered if the gesture was supposed to be threatening but when she saw Henry's face she realised there was nothing but frustration.

If there was anger, then it was only directed toward himself.

He bowed his head, examining his hands, as if he might've cut himself.

He hadn't.

He shifted his attention back onto Elena.

"I'm sorry," he said. "Sometimes I just can't believe the things I've done ... the things I *did* ... I understand that you — and many others — think I'm a monster. That I'm some unstoppable, destructive force.

But I want to tell you, even if they're only words, that I *have* changed. I'm not the person I once was."

The breeze blew chillier still.

Elena's teeth chattered together.

Her heart beat against the back of her throat.

"Can you understand that?" Henry said, on the brink of shouting. Demanding a reply.

Elena retreated a couple of steps.

Apparently noticing the effect of his words on her, Henry softened his tone, and then repeated, "Can you understand?"

Elena met his eye for the longest time.

She thought about the night they'd spent together.

She thought about the *blood*.

She thought about the embarrassment.

She thought about the *fear* ... and here was Henry ... *apologising!*

"I'm not asking for forgiveness," he said. "I am only asking you to listen. The person who ... *did* those things no longer exists. There's no reason to *be afraid.*"

Elena couldn't keep the snark out of her reply.

"Who says I'm *afraid?*"

Henry held very still. And then, out of nowhere, he lunged at her, shouted, "*Boo!*"

Elena flinched, retreating a few steps.

Her calves brushed up against a low wall behind her.

Henry wasn't smiling at the reaction he'd evoked.

In fact, he was grimacing.

At the *reputation* he'd built.

There was silence until Elena couldn't take it any longer.

"You were my first," she said.

A strange smile crept across her lips.

The smile was strange because she felt close to tears.

She forced herself onward.

"You're not the only one who's changed, Henry — "

"Harry," he replied. "Please call me Harry."

Elena sidestepped this interjection.

For her he would *always* be "Henry".

She continued, "I remember feeling so special when you asked me over. Like I was living some beautiful dream." She shook her head. "The night before, I hardly slept. I couldn't believe it was real." She drew in a breath and her shoulders slouched with a sigh as she exhaled. "Childhood crushes are funny things, Henry." She examined his features, seeing the slight flinch as she refused to bend to his whim. "They're *powerful* things ... more powerful than they're given credit." Out of nowhere, she snorted a laugh. "I mean, there was a time when I clearly recall thinking that if there ever existed a possibility of the two of us being together then I would be willing to *kill* for it."

Henry didn't react.

He only met her eyes.

Realising she was finished, he crushed his lips together and looked out across the garden to Goonherth Bay beyond. "I'm sorry," was all he said.

Elena turned her own gaze to the bay. "Me too, Henry."

JOCK

7.35 PM, SUNDAY

J ock draped his jacket over his shoulders as he brought the door shut behind him.

He resisted the urge to take one last peep.

Such urges were the hallmark of amateur killers.

The ones who never fully realised their plans.

The ones who never quite finished the job they'd set out to do.

Like all the other boys at school, Jock had fantasised about Jasmine Everglade.

He could still remember how he would lie in bed at night thinking about her.

Before the *accident* he would stroke himself ... *down there* ... and think about how he was disgracing his parents; how he was revealing himself to be nothing more than a disgusting animal; fit only to be slaughtered.

Jock paced along the landing, passing various doorways.

He heard the *buzz* of conversation downstairs.

Laughter.

The *clink* of glasses.

This was a reminder of the *Greatest Time of their Lives ...*

But not for Jock.

Jock could still feel Jasmine's touch.

It had been different to how he had imagined.

He had believed her skin would be hot ... and yet she had been cold.

Freezing cold.

And it had been how he always felt whenever he was with women.

That unshakeable feeling that he was in an examination room.

That they wanted to *learn* about his mutilated body.

That they wanted to find out how to give him *pleasure*.

But there was no way for them to give him pleasure.

Not now.

He had tried everything.

And everything had failed.

He felt the steady weight of the flick knife in the inside pocket of his jacket.

He so wanted to whip it out.

To swipe it across his own throat.

To take his own life.

But not yet.

Not *yet*.

He paced onward, thinking through his next move.

He would simply return to the drawing room.

He would take a seat and wait.

As if nothing had happened.

Right as Jock was about to set foot on the staircase — right when he was about to descend to the "party" — he paused.

The door across from him drew his attention.

He breathed in.

Exhaled.

Then trod toward it.

The door was slightly ajar.

All the other doors were closed.

He supposed this was why it had caught his eye.

He breathed very gently now — paying attention to any sound.

From within the room, he was certain he could sense a human presence.

The *beating* of a heart.

Jock peeped in through the crack of the open door.

He made out the bed within.

The *four-poster* bed.

There was nothing like a *four-poster* bed to say *nouveau riche*.

Not that he had ever been what he considered *riche* ... old or new.

He glanced around, managing to convince himself that someone might be watching. But there was no one.

He observed the four-poster bed within the room.

There was nothing for it.

He had come this far.

And he wouldn't back out now.

He stepped into the room.

Allowed the darkness to swarm over him.

STEPHEN
7.39 PM, SUNDAY

As Stephen sat alone at the piano keys, he could feel a constant pounding at the side of his face. He peered over the top of the sleek black body of the piano, and out through the windows to the garden and the bay beyond.

He had always loved the sound of silence.

It was what he had loved so much about performing.

Whether in a concert hall or a recording studio, he lived for those few seconds of complete silence just before he commenced playing. He loved to hear the sound of the audience, or studio engineer, suddenly becoming quiet.

Standing reverent.

Anticipating.

Some nights, he would pause for five or ten seconds, absorbing the sensation.

If he attempted to draw out that period of time any longer coughing or the rustling of programmes or the shuffling of feet would destroy the illusion. For him — *for Stephen Foldes* — the prime moment of the concert was just before he started.

That was the *perfect* time.

... And then he would go and ruin it all.

As he breathed in, he listened to the gentle, low-level chatter of those in the drawing room where the party was taking place.

The Crosses had been almost static in the previous months — no movement at all.

Everything tonight seemed to be unfurling within a dream.

A sudden rush of frenzied activity.

And that, he supposed, was why he had agreed to play.

He had seen no reason to refuse Joanne or Elena; a pair of *very pleasant* girls.

And now he had returned to the silence.

To that dear, ever-lasting, profound silence.

Stephen heard the sound of the staircase creaking.

Someone coming downstairs.

He gave a wry smile.

He supposed school reunions had a habit of stirring up long-forgotten, but ill-buried, feelings. He remained straight-backed on the piano stool another few moments before rising.

It was time for him to return to the party.

JOANNE

7.42 PM, SUNDAY

When Joanne looked over the faces present in the drawing room, she felt a skitter run up her spine. There was something about this scene which swept her back to her childhood — which swept her back to her school days.

Although she was certain it would've shocked many people to have known the truth, she had never felt all that at ease in crowds. She had never felt fully *herself* when with other people. She'd always been most at ease alone in her bedroom. She had always enjoyed the quiet, peeling back the pages of her notebook and doing homework.

She had never found homework to be a chore.

She enjoyed the mechanical workings of her brain.

The satisfying scrawl of handwriting on paper.

She eyed Jock, sitting across the room.

He had returned a couple of minutes ago.

She was somewhat surprised he had been invited at all and that he had accepted the invitation. But he was here ... And then there was the matter that he'd recently stumbled out of the drawing room with a — *clearly drunk* — Jasmine Everglade.

That was a conquest, indeed.

Henry Foldes's childhood sweetheart.

Did Jock even *have* the ability to be with a woman?

Had Jasmine sent him packing in swift order?

Since Jock wouldn't meet her eye, Joanne turned her attention to other matters.

The absence of Jasmine.

Last time Joanne had seen Jasmine, she had been worse for wear.

How much she'd had to drink, Joanne had found difficult to say.

That was the thing with people you didn't know very well.

You could never *quite* tell how much was a psychological reaction.

It was conceivable that Jasmine had simply been *acting* drunk, of course.

Because she'd seemed that way.

Looking around the room to the chattering, happy faces she decided she should go and check on Jasmine. She might need someone to hold back her hair.

A kind of show of female solidarity.

Joanne ventured out of the dining room, passing by a queasy-looking Edward Wanton. He was slumped in one of the armchairs, gently rocking from side to side. She wondered if Edward might be one of those men who required a minder — a wife or girlfriend — to *nurture* him. But Joanne would take care of Jasmine first.

That was her priority.

Once out of the drawing room, Joanne couldn't help but find herself drawn by the bright white light strobing out of the kitchen. Half-blinded by the light, she nearly bumped into Stephen Foldes coming the other way. He apologised and then continued on his way, toward the drawing room.

As she watched him go, the music he'd been playing returned to her mind.

It had been so ... *beautiful.*

... So *mournful.*

Joanne wasn't all that well acquainted with classical music, but she wondered if Stephen Foldes was known for any compositions with a somewhat *brighter* tone. Then again, she didn't suppose the current situation — what with his wife up in bed, near death — was particularly conducive to "happy" music.

In the kitchen, Joanne explored the small toilet off to the side, wondering whether she might find Jasmine here. But the toilet was unoccupied. Some motion through the window attracted her attention. She held her hand up to the cool glass to shield the glare from the lights inside and peered out.

The statue.

A couple of people beside it. Although she couldn't make out much in the gloom, neither of them looked like Jasmine.

She withdrew from the window, turning back to the kitchen.

Jasmine wasn't here.

Joanne's gaze came to rest on one of the drawers.

She slid it open.

Took in the contents.

Cutlery.

Knives and forks.

With a smile, she made to close the drawer.

Why had she felt compelled to open it?

Something caught the light:

A chef's *knife.*

She stared at the blade for a long moment.

Tried to pin down the exact thought process as it bounced about her mind.

She wanted to take the knife out.

She wanted to take it *with* her.

Why?

But before Joanne could fully understand her thought process, she removed the knife. Held it down at her thigh.

The knife was bulky.

It rested against her hip.

She found herself thinking about one of those phrases from her childhood, about how she was never to run with scissors ... and when it came to knives ... she was just plain supposed to leave them alone.

Well, she certainly hadn't left *this* knife alone.

Joanne left the kitchen and ventured upstairs.

As she passed along the corridor, she was conscious of being close to Henry's dying mother. She felt a feeling akin to trespassing. And, well, she supposed that was what she was doing. She had no right to be here. She had *no right* to be on the upper floors at all ... no matter what'd passed between her and Henry the night before.

That was in the past.

Something that would never occur again.

She pictured herself in her mind's eye ... she must look like some psychopath ... a *serial* killer ... stalking her way through a darkened mansion.

Unbeknownst to the party taking place below.

She remembered her task, that she was supposed to be tracking down Jasmine.

She could hardly call out her name.

She would disturb Henry's mother.

Instead, she took to pressing her ear up against each door.

Listening for any activity within.

She opened a few doors as she went, hoping against hope that they wouldn't lead to Henry's mother's bedroom. And finally she found Jasmine.

Unlike the other rooms she had seen, the furniture wasn't shrouded by dust sheets and blankets. This room — a *guest* room — was made up ready for someone to spend the night. As she stood in the doorway, Jasmine's sleeping form illuminated by the moonlight which streamed in through the window, she felt a sudden thrill pass through her blood. And she felt herself being drawn back to that night ... to *that* night again.

It had been the party to end school.

And it had taken place here — at The Crosses.

Joanne remembered arriving.

Of course it had been after the "official" celebration. Throughout the course of the day she had snuck various drinks; laying to rest once and for all the "good girl" image she had upheld throughout school. It had been an open secret that Henry Foldes had designs on her. Another open secret was that Henry Foldes had slept with just about every girl in their school year.

There had been fear.

And there had been desire.

Back then it had been so difficult to separate the two ... to know which one was *excitement* and which one was natural instinct:

A *warning*.

When Joanne had arrived to The Crosses, she had been struck by its bulky rectangular shape. If it hadn't been for the warm lighting at each of the windows, it would've been a foreboding sight. But because of the alcohol she had ingested she found herself unmoved. It'd been the first house party she'd ever attended. And she'd been taken off guard by her fellow students packing the corridors.

Overwhelmed by the constant buzz of chatter.

The *body* heat.

Everyone had a plastic cup in their hand.

Joanne had soon found herself separated from her friends. She wasn't entirely sure how it had happened but it *had* ...

One minute she'd been hanging off their heels and the next they'd vanished.

At the time the thought of there being anything like a conspiracy hadn't occurred to Joanne. It'd been then, of course, with the sound of Stephen Foldes's piano playing thick in her ears, that she had found herself facing Jasmine, Henry's girlfriend.

Before Joanne could do anything to prevent it, she had felt the hard rim of a bottle against her lips. It had knocked painfully a couple of times against her teeth. When she first sensed the overpoweringly *hot* and *bitter* liquid upon her tongue, she had spluttered. Jasmine had acted as if she was a nurse administering medicine to an uncooperative patient. She had taken her time, waited for Joanne to collect herself, and then shoved the bottle at her once again.

It was then that the world had started to blur.

The sequence of events which'd followed were difficult for Joanne to trace.

She was aware of Jasmine leading her by the hand.

Jasmine had led her into a toilet, stood with her while Joanne "got her head together". She couldn't remember vomiting, although she might well have done. She had drunk a glass or two of water before allowing Jasmine to lead her off into the house, along constantly moving corridors, into an anonymous-looking guestroom.

It might even have been *this* guestroom.

Where Joanne stood now.

Where she could make out Jasmine's reclining body.

Silhouetted by the moonlight.

She clasped her eyes shut as she ran through the events in her mind once again.

As she thought through the sensation she'd experienced upon waking.

The *pain*.

Sharp ... impossible to bear ... *stinging*.

She had been lying beside Jasmine.

Naked.

She wasn't sure if Jasmine had been naked too.

Her memory was fuzzy.

But she had smelled the blood on the air.

That bitter, coppery odour.

... Could she smell it now?

Memory was a funny thing.

A *powerful* thing.

She had looked to where she had felt the pain.

Seen Jasmine with her head bowed.

Between her legs.

Joanne recalled asking Jasmine what she was doing.

Asking *where* she was ...

Where *they* were ...

Jasmine had held her finger to her lips.

Told her to be silent.

But Joanne had snapped upright.

Sat up straight.

Despite her drunkenness, she had overpowered Jasmine.

Seen the knife she held clasped in her fist.

Even in the gloom, she had made out the dark trickle of blood on her inner thigh.

And she could tell the intention.

Just what Jasmine had been *in the middle* of doing.

She had been working her way slowly inward.

Ready to ... to ...

It didn't bear thinking about.

Joanne turned her mind to other things.

Snapped her attention back to the present.

Back to *now*.

This was her chance, wasn't it?

This was *her* chance for vengeance ...

All she needed to do was give the sleeping woman a slight *nick*.

Just like the one Joanne had.

Just like the one *Elena* had shown her.

Joanne stood there, for the longest time, smelling the blood in her nostrils, eyeing Jasmine's sleeping form. And then, slowly, she backed out of the room.

This was wrong.

She *couldn't* do this ... no.

No, no, no, no, NO!

She allowed the knife to slip through her fingers.

It clattered at her feet.
She expected Jasmine to stir.
But she continued to sleep.
To *sleep away* ...
Joanne looked her over once more and then drew the door shut.
It was time for her to get back to the party.

JOCK

8.05 PM, SUNDAY

J ock felt as if he'd been swept up in some sort of tornado as he sat to one side in the drawing room. He took in the couples dancing drunkenly. They twirled about one another. Their smiles were like gashes ...

Gashes.

Jock could still feel his heart humming within his chest.

Some motion caught his eye in the doorway.

Henry Foldes.

On instinct, his eyes dropped to Henry's hands where he held a tumbler of whisky filled to the brim. Henry was supporting himself against the doorframe, clearly struggling with the quantity of drink he had consumed.

It made Jock sick to think his *childhood* bully might somehow have his own problems. His own demons.

What *right* did he have?

As Jock sat drinkless in the armchair, he wondered if he could simply venture out of the house. If he could *leave* this place behind.

He had only to hop in his car.

Drive back to the bed-and-breakfast.

Pick up his luggage.

And return "home".

It was strange to think the daily grind would resume on Monday.

That he could forget all that had happened here, in Goonherth Bay.

In reality, though, he knew it was impossible.

He could never forget.

He had already tried to do so, and failed ... over and over again.

Right now, Jock was finding it difficult to gauge the passing time.

Had it really been two hours since he had ... *killed* ... Jasmine?

He had been unable to resist.

The opportunity had simply presented itself.

Perhaps there was something wrong with him.

Something *fatally* wrong.

Murderers, like him, were not ordinary human beings.

They were always damaged in some way.

Jock and Henry's eyes crossed briefly.

Then Henry looked elsewhere.

Jock knew Henry recognised him.

Even a brute like Henry would surely have difficulty forgetting a boy he had castrated. Was that the reason for the whisky? So Henry might forget the nightmares he "suffered"? Was that a good sign? Some suggestion of responsibility?

Even repentance?

It made no difference.

No difference to *Jock*.

He was permanently damaged.

Physically damaged.

Forever and ever.

Henry peeled away from the doorframe.

This was his opportunity.

There might never be another chance.

With a vague nod to the ever-queasy, semi-sentient Edward sitting across from him, Jock rose from his seat and headed out of the drawing room.

He had his prey in his sights.

And it would not escape.

JOANNE

8.11 PM, SUNDAY

Joanne left the kitchen and ventured out across the gravel path which led away from the house. More than once, she glanced back over her shoulder.

Her gut stirred.

Was someone following?

She couldn't tell.

Did Henry have some means of tracking her?

She turned the corner to find Elena sitting on the low wall beside the cherubic statue. Elena was looking in the direction of the bay, captivated by the calm water.

The rain had stopped falling and there was a certain stillness in the air.

Joanne sensed the thickening humidity.

She took a deep breath, trying to rid herself of the thoughts of what she had just done. How she had eyed the sleeping Jasmine and thought about mutilating her.

Mutilating Jasmine the same way Jasmine had mutilated *her*.

But she hadn't.

Did that make her better than Jasmine?

Did it hand her the moral high ground?

"Are you okay?" Joanne asked.

Elena didn't look around right away.

She remained fixated upon the ocean.

Joanne rounded Elena, stood before her, blocking her view.

Finally Elena looked up.

She was crying.

"Shall we go home?" Joanne asked.

Elena held still.

Didn't respond.

In the end, she nodded.

Joanne smiled and offered her hand to help her up.

But Elena remained where she was.

"What ... what's the matter?" Joanne asked.

"Earlier, when I showed you what ... *he* did ..."

Of course Joanne recalled the scar Elena had shown her on her inner thigh.

Just like hers ...

Was Elena going to reveal some other sickening truth about Henry?

What did it matter to Joanne anyway?

Last night had been an ending — an ending which should've taken place years before. And it would have done. If only Jasmine hadn't attacked her ... then there never would've been any reason for ending up here at this very statue with the two of them saying goodbye for the last time.

Joanne had wanted to stay.

She had wanted to spend the night with Henry.

But she had had to attend to her wound.

Elena continued, "In the music room. Were you holding something back?"

Joanne met Elena's eye.

Why wasn't it easy for her to tell the truth?

To put what had happened into words?

Did she think that telling someone now might ruin her "good girl" reputation?

Even *fifteen years* later ...?

The past hung about her neck.

Weighing her down.

Now was the time to lighten the load.

If she valued her relationship with Elena at all — if she valued the honesty they had built up — she had to tell her.

No, more than that.

She had to *show* her.

She set her foot on the edge of the statue base.

Slowly, she eased the hem of her dress up her thigh.

She tremored to think what she was doing.

She had hidden this for so long — just as Elena had.

As Joanne revealed her scar, she studied Elena's face, taking in her reaction.

Trying to gauge what thoughts might be moving through her brain.

There was no need for words.

They both knew ... the two of them were victims of Henry Foldes.

"It was Jasmine," Joanne said. "She was the one who did it." Something caught in her throat. "Jealousy ... something like that."

"*Jasmine?*" Elena echoed. "Not Henry?"

Joanne nodded.

Over her shoulder, Joanne heard the crunch of the gravel pathway.

She flinched, quickly allowed her dress to fall back down.

She followed Elena's gaze, to the person standing nearby.

Even in near darkness, Joanne could tell who it was:

Edward Wanton.

She took in his staggering posture.

His pale complexion.

Edward had one of those faces which could be recognised in darkness.

Perhaps only ever fully understood in darkness.

A chilly breeze cut through the warming air and Joanne felt her skin pucker into goose pimples.

Edward took a step toward them.

A lazy smile hung from his lips.

He had a slight stagger to his gait.

Joanne thought it something of a marvel he was standing at all.

When he drew close enough for them to make out his drunken voice, he nodded to her dress, to her thigh. "I'd like to show you something."

Joanne shifted to Elena and then looked back to Edward.

She waited a few heartbeats.

And then said, "What?"

Edward only gave a wry grin by way of response. He produced a glass filled with some liquor or other from down at his side and took a swig.

Then he grinned wider still. "Come inside and see."

HENRY

8.14 PM, SUNDAY

Harry's mother's bedroom was cold.

Ice cold.

He trod the creaking floorboards, drawing closer to the bed.

The rain had stopped drumming against the windowpanes twenty minutes ago.

As he approached the bed, he felt as if he was violating this space.

As if he was violating his *mother's* space.

And yet ... he couldn't bring himself to leave.

If these truly were his mother's final moments on the Earth then she surely wouldn't begrudge sharing them with her own child?

Then again, he and his mother had never been close.

More like distant relatives at times.

Each in their own world.

Lost.

The darkness wrapped about Harry like a damp cloak.

A shudder ran through him.

He clenched his teeth, wished the unpleasant sensation away.

He could go fetch the jacket he had left hanging off the back of one of the drawing room chairs. But something told him it was too late. That there was *no* time to waste.

He crept closer to the bed.

Eyed his mother.

As before she was buried beneath her duvet, blankets on top. When his eyes became accustomed to the dark he began to make out the basic features of her face.

Sunken eye sockets.

Mournful cheekbones.

Frown lines leathered into the forehead.

He sat on the edge of the bland mattress.

Although he craved warmth he would find none here.

He reached out for his mother's arm, trailing out beneath the blankets.

He stroked her papery skin.

Felt the clammy, earthy coolness.

A tremor ran through his heart.

Was he too late?

Had ... *it* already happened?

Harry leaned into his mother.

His breath felt impossibly hot in the frigid air.

When he spoke, it was as if he was speaking to himself. "... Mum?" he said.

He waited for a response.

Any response.

None came.

He tried again.

"Mum?"

Still nothing.

His fingertips traced the underside of her arm, almost unconsciously. When they reached her wrist they paused, checking the pulse.

Nothing.

He shifted his grip slightly.

Nothing.

He slipped his fingers further along.

And waited the longest time.

He felt the weakest of beats.

The strength of a feather.

But it was *something*.

In response, Harry squeezed his mother's wrist tightly.

He leaned into her.

Reached out for her stringy, tightly coiled hair.

Gave it a stroke.

He felt the texture against his skin.

A shudder passed through his stomach.

"Mum?" he asked again.

This time she flickered an eyelid.

She regarded him from the bottoms of her eyes.

Harry's heart slowed right down.

All of a sudden, it began to pound in his throat.

Thick, heavy palpitations.

He was afraid.

Afraid of this place.

... Of home.

It was better for him to return to the city.

To go *now*.

As Harry readied to rise, he felt a tight grip on his forearm.

He turned back to his mother.

Her lips were parted.

She was *trying* to say something.

Harry held back a few seconds. And then he leaned towards her.

He brought his ear close to her lips.

He heard a rasping sound from the back of her throat.

And then finally two words:

"... Stay ... away ... stay ... away."

Perplexed, Harry drew back. As he did so, he took in her face.

Her features appeared to have frozen.

Had life finally left her?

Forever?

Slowly, Harry's mind made sense of what his mother had said.

It was the strangest feeling.

As if a whirlpool had appeared within his brain.

Within the whirlpool circled the words she had spoken.

Again and *again.*

Stay away ... stay away ... STAY AWAY!

It was now that Harry felt the tension across his stomach.

It was now that he felt the entire room spin.

He shrugged off his mother's grip.

Rose to his feet.

When he inhaled, it came as a gasp.

He simply couldn't find the air.

He *gulped.*

Staggered back from the bed.

Still facing his dead mother, unable to wrench his eyes away, he fumbled for the doorknob behind him. But only found the wall.

Finally, he gathered the strength to look away.

He turned his attention to escape.

To *getting away* from this place.

It was then that the darkness took on form.

A *figure* emerged from the gloom.

It confused Harry for several moments.

Some part of his brain succeeded in convincing him he was alone in the house.

That he hadn't asked all these "strangers" back here.

When he finally took stock of the darkness, he realised it was no stranger.

... It was his father.

Just as he had been earlier, he wore a tuxedo.

In the darkness, Harry couldn't help but summon the idea he had somehow been transported backstage; that he was waiting for his father to go out on stage ...

For some concert.

As if it was necessary — or perhaps it was merely a reaction borne out of shock — his father said, "She's gone, Harry."

Harry felt his whole body tremble.

A single tear squeezed free from the corner of his eye.

It rolled down his cheek.

"... I know," Harry managed to reply.

His father put his arms about him.

He drew Harry into his chest.

Harry felt his father's lips right by his ear.

His *warm* breath.

"You would never guess who I found here," his father said.

Harry was confused by the statement.

He analysed it.

Tried to work out if his father was expressing his thoughts in some metaphorical way. If his father was going to start into some *spiritual* explanation.

But, no ... Harry was *certain* his meaning was more literal than that.

Gently, he pried himself free of his father's embrace.

He blinked several times, doing his best to clear his daze.

Doing his best to bring the world back.

And then he saw him ... standing in the corner, like some archangel.

An angel of death.

He took stock of the long black hair, and the expression devoid of emotion.

And he noted the syringe he held down at his waist.

Jock Jones.

It was then that the pieces clicked into place.

As if it was necessary to establish the facts absolutely, Harry returned to his mother's side, his fear vanquished for the time being. He examined the underside of her arm. And saw the black bead of blood there.

Where the needle had penetrated her skin.

Harry acted out of instinct.

He rushed Jock.

Right at the last moment, Jock sidestepped, and Harry met the wall with a *thwack*.

Rubbing his skull, Harry admitted to himself that he had had his fair share of drink this evening. He wasn't able to keep a firm hold on the dimensions surrounding him.

He caught sight of Jock again, but this time stumbled and tumbled to the floor.

Lying on his back, stunned, staring upward, his gaze settled upon his mother lying in bed. And then his father dressed in his tuxedo.

He waited for him to say something.

He waited for him to *do* something ... and yet he just stood calmly by.

As if what had just happened — what was *happening* — was the most normal thing in the whole world.

"It needed to be done," his father said. "Her last wish was to *see* you." He pressed his lips so tightly together that they were pallid, bloodless. "Once accomplished, the kindest thing was to allow her to slip away."

Harry took a few moments to gather himself together.

To *try* and make sense of the situation.

He glared at Jock, as if he was going to give him an answer.

From where Harry lay, Jock was a giant.

Towering over him.

Harry supposed it must've been deeply satisfying for Jock to turn the tables.

Harry thought about that moment all those years ago.

When he had stood over Jock.

When he watched the others castrate him.

Did Harry have any regrets?

... Only one ... instead of castrating Jock, he should've *killed* him.

Maybe he could kill him *now*.

Harry noted the knife Jock held in his other fist.

Moonlight glinted off the blade.

Harry felt his body go tight all over.

His heart hammered his ribs.

What was this?

What *the hell* was this?

He looked to his father, still standing by the door. "Dad?" he said. "*Dad?!*"

But Jock was already bearing down on Harry, and it was all Harry could do to scuttle backward, away from the advancing man.

Away from that rancid all-consuming halitosis.

But there *was* no escape.

The door was in the other direction.

When Harry felt the tip of the blade press his throat he knew it was all over.

He had never imagined, when he had arrived — when he had *returned* home — that he might be living out his past few hours. But, then again, if life had taught him anything at all then it was that it was *full* of surprises.

... *Surprise.*

ELENA
8.19 PM, SUNDAY

E lena had been reluctant to return to the house.

She had wanted — more than anything — to go home.

Parenthood had played havoc with her stamina.

She now found it unnatural to stay up much beyond seven o'clock at night.

She could simply no longer *manage*.

But under Edward and Joanne's pleading she *had* returned.

They had decided on the music room.

From the looks of things, Elena wasn't the only parent among her school year.

Many others had headed home apparently no longer interested in burning the candle at both ends. When she had peeped into the drawing room, as they'd ventured onto the music room, she had seen it was near deserted.

Only a scattering of people had remained.

Drinking the liquor cabinet dry.

Joanne flipped on the lights in the music room.

It felt as if she was invading — as if she didn't *belong* here.

But of course *none* of them belonged here.

Did all recluses' houses feel this way?

Did they all feel this strange?

Elena made an effort not to focus on the framed concert posters which hung on the walls. She didn't want to see Stephen Foldes's smile.

That smile.

It sent a shudder up her spine and her stomach sinking through the floor.

Although Joanne and Edward sat without delay, Elena hovered a good few moments ... toying with the idea of taking a seat.

Finally, she did.

But she kept her distance from Joanne and Edward.

Strangely, it felt like she'd been transported back to school — as if the old allegiances were alive and well. As if Elena was very much an *outsider*.

Elena was becoming uncontrollably anxious, waiting for the others to say *something* ... waiting for Edward to reveal what he had to *show* them.

She heard footsteps approaching, out in the corridor.

Stephen Foldes appeared in the doorway.

He was dressed in his tuxedo, as he had been earlier.

Without a word, he took a seat at the piano stool and commenced playing.

Just like before, the music was slow, mournful.

It wasn't often that Elena felt herself affected by music — she had never really been *that* into music — but there was an undeniable quality to the melody which stirred something deep inside. It was as if Stephen Foldes operated *beyond* music.

He could manipulate thoughts, emotions, like an actor.

She supposed transporting an audience was the duty of the performer.

And he was certainly transporting them now.

As Stephen Foldes played, quietly enough for them to be able to hold a conversation, someone else appeared in the doorway.

It took Elena a few moments to work out who it was:

Jock Jones.

She hadn't seen him for ages.

In truth, she had thought he'd gone.

Apparently not ...

As the piano music swilled, Elena studied Jock.

Gangly, stringy black hair ... *greasy*.

Back slightly bent as he hunched forward.

There was something about him.

Something about the way he *held* himself.

How he lurked there.

Did he have something to tell them?

She cast her mind back to that ridiculous meeting the night before.

When she had bandied around the notion of "revenge".

Just *what* had she been thinking?

Why couldn't she let the past go?

Why couldn't she let what *Henry* had done to her go?

She thought back to the scar which Joanne had shown her.

The one which matched hers.

Joanne had said Jasmine had done it ...

But why?

And why had Henry done it to Elena?

And how had they got away with it?

... Was everyone as ashamed as she was?

Too *afraid* to come forward?

Edward and Jock nodded to one another and Jock trod into the room. He took a seat nearby. For a few minutes, they all sat still, listening to the gorgeous music Stephen Foldes played. When he came to the end of the current piece, Elena broke the silence that followed their clapping. "Where's Max?"

She addressed the question to Jock, of course.

Even though Jock and Max hadn't been friends at school, Elena had sort of grouped them together in their adult lives. As if through their childhood suffering at the hands of Henry they somehow shared a connection. It was an unfair judgement, but, then again, Elena couldn't prevent her unconscious mind from making these leaps of logic.

"Don't know," Jock replied, abruptly.

"Perhaps he went home," Edward added.

Elena couldn't help but note that Edward's tone was cleaner cut now. She wondered if whatever drug or drink had been swilling about his veins was loosening its hold on him. There was something else to his voice, too.

Something she didn't much like.

Then again, she had never much liked Edward.

"What did you want to show us?" Joanne asked Edward.

Elena met Joanne's gaze, looked to Edward.

Edward became somewhat coy.

He folded his arms over his chest, as if to hold onto whatever secret he had to reveal for just another few seconds. Finally, though, he got to his feet.

It was a surreal scene.

The dreary piano melody.

Edward undoing his belt … allowing his trousers to slip down past his waist.

Elena couldn't look away.

Edward stood before them in only his underwear.

It was a tight-fitting pair.

With a practised motion, he hooked his thumbs over the elastic waistband and eased his underwear down his hips.

Maybe if Elena had been stone-cold sober she would've averted her gaze.

However, a sort of drunken haze had set in over her mind.

Everything seemed to have gone fuzzy about the edges.

And she *couldn't* look away.

As she took in the sight, she felt herself being swept back.

To all of those stories — to all of those *rumours* ... to the things Henry did to women ... to *girls* ... the things Henry did to *other boys*.

Edward's underwear covered nothing but smoothed-over scarred tissue.

He had no penis.

No testicles.

Although Elena was deeply aware of Edward staring intently at her — and at Joanne — clearly wanting them to deliver their verdict on his mutilation, Elena could think of nothing to say.

What *was* there to say?

She looked away not out of a sense of horror but because she expected Jock to reciprocate. Would he confirm or deny the rumours from their school days?

Jock, however, did not remove his trousers. If he did have something to show them then he had no intention of "putting it on display".

Apparently content they had seen all they *needed* to see, Edward dragged his underwear — and his trousers — back up. As he buckled his belt, he spoke in a low grumbling voice almost lost among the meanderings of Stephen Foldes's piano playing.

"We have all been affected," Edward said. "By what Henry *chose* to do."

Here Elena couldn't help but break in. "But from what I heard you were ... *involved* ... you know ... with the *things* Henry got up to."

Edward stayed still.

So did Jock.

Finally, Edward responded. "You know so little about *what* Henry wanted ... about *what* was going on."

Maybe it was the alcohol or perhaps just the ridiculousness of the situation.

Elena shifted her attention onto Stephen Foldes, apparently off in his own world, playing his tunes. He had his eyes closed.

Then she looked back to Edward and Jock.

There was ... *something* going on.
They seemed so calm.
So *unbelievably* calm.
Then she glanced at Joanne.
She looked just as confused as Elena felt.

HENRY
8.30 PM, SUNDAY

H arry came around to the stench of blood.
His blood.

He felt the warmth flowing from his throat, matting his chest.

He gasped — *long and hard* — attempting to draw breath.

Then he opened his eyes.

Found himself surrounded by darkness.

He waited out the seconds — his eyes growing accustomed to the gloom.

When he realised he was lying on his front, he used his elbow to prop himself up onto his side. It took almost all of his energy to catch his breath.

To find the requisite strength to continue.

He felt faint.

His blood thin.

When he reached up for his throat, he could feel the blood still oozing out.

He had to stop the bleeding.

With shaking hands, he worked to undo his shirt buttons. When he had removed his shirt, he bundled it into a ball and held it to the wound. As he applied pressure, he couldn't help but give a grim smile. He was certain Jock felt a *grand* sense of accomplishment. He had *one-upped* Harry ... at last.

He had managed to *kill* Harry.

The blood loss made him chuckle hysterically.

It threatened to steal his senses away completely.

The situation seemed so *funny*, though ... so ridiculous.

More than a dozen times, Harry felt the darkness threatening to swill over him.

Each time he felt himself nodding off, he slapped his cheek, waking himself up.

He was a fighter.

He'd *always* been a fighter.

Everything he'd built — away from Goonherth Bay — he had built *himself*.

And he would be damned if he allowed some weedy little shit with a childhood grudge to take it away from him.

He would be *damned*.

He eased himself up against the wall. He was aware that he left a bloody smear upon everything he touched. That he was leaving a trail.

Once, when he glanced down, he noted a puddle of blood — his *own* blood.

Feeling it turn his stomach just to look at it, he shifted his attention away.

He had to keep his thoughts moving forward.

Harry staggered against the wall, keeping himself upright. When he reached the door, he turned the knob, found that it was stiff.

Locked.

Feeling the wooziness returning, he took several deep breaths.

He tried to get his thoughts straight again.

Tried to get what'd *happened* straight.

And because he couldn't avoid it — because it might well prove to be the last time he ever got the chance — he looked at his mother's dead body.

She lay there, blanket pulled up to her chin.

Lifeless face.

Clay complexion.

Someone had drawn the curtain so moonlight flooded the room.

Almost a supernatural sight.

And — *strangely* — one which reaffirmed Harry's longing for life.

His longing to *live*.

Harry thought through his options.

He could beat on the door.

Hope someone would come to his rescue.

... But that might only summon Jock Jones.

Bring him back to finish the job.

Even though Harry would've fancied himself against Jock on a level playing field, this situation was anything but.

Jock was armed.

And Harry wasn't.

It was then, casting his glance over his dead mother for the final time, that his gaze came to rest on the window. The moon outside.

A promise of freedom.

Harry approached the window, saw he could slide it open.

The gravel driveway swayed below him.

A drainpipe ran up the exterior wall beside the window.

It would be a tough task.

Although Harry made sure to keep himself in shape — he was meticulous in his discipline in getting down the gym at least five times a week — he knew it would've been a challenge even if he'd had all his senses about him.

If he had still possessed his *full* strength.

Now, though, he would be forced to descend in his current condition.

This, he supposed, was survival.

This, he supposed, was his *test*.

As he perched on the windowsill, he felt the cool breeze blowing back his hair.

In the distance, he made out Goonherth Bay, the moonlight playing in the ripples of the ocean. He wondered if after this was all over he might catch a ship and simply ... *sail away.*

Could he disappear so easily?

Could he "be gone" so simply?

The thought throbbed at his forehead like a headache.

An irresistible enticement.

Why not?

His own father had betrayed him ...

JOANNE

8.37 PM, SUNDAY

Joanne glanced at Elena again, meeting her eye briefly.

There was a note of danger now.

Or had it been there the whole time?

She looked to Edward and then Jock.

The two of them sitting opposite.

Stephen Foldes continued to play the incessantly sad, incredibly beautiful, music.

Did Henry possess something of his father's gift?

An *artistic* urge buried deep within.

Was he really the cutthroat business man he painted himself as?

She would never know.

Because once this evening was over she would have nothing more to do with him.

The prospect seemed both reassuring and *devastating* ...

Joanne waited for Edward to open up about what had gone on back at school.

She just wanted the truth, whatever its implications.

When Stephen Foldes ceased playing, it was like a thunderstorm subsiding.

A shudder ran up Joanne's spine.

Stephen Foldes sat straight-backed at the piano stool.

As if Joanne had asked him for an explanation, he began to speak.

"I take full responsibility, of course," he said. "Henry always seemed so ... *directionless*. He was popular at school, but he never *did* anything with that power."

Joanne's gut tightened.

Her blood ran hot.

Then impossibly cold.

He went on, "He needed a shove. He needed some *poking*." He bowed his head to the piano, shaking his head at the keys. "I never thought he would take my words literally, obviously. I never thought he would take my advice and use it to hurt others." He threw his hand off in Jock and Edward's direction, as if they were mere props on a stage. "But, after all that went on, we have to admit *one* thing — if *only* one thing ..."

In mid-thought, Stephen Foldes slipped away into silence.

Joanne raised her voice. "And what's that?"

Stephen Foldes continued to stare at the sleek ebony body of his piano. He smiled slightly. "It proves what celebrity can do for a person. The sorts of hooks it lets one off."

Joanne was certain this was a joke.

"I decided to end my touring," Stephen Foldes went on, "to bring an end to my concert-playing days. I thought it would work better for Henry ... that I would have more of a chance to raise my own son. We thought we would keep him shielded from all the ... the *lewdness* of a big city; of the more unsavoury trimmings which would accompany my career." He shrugged his shoulders, not in a carefree way, more out of exasperation. He sighed. "But the boy just had *wickedness* in him."

As silence loomed large once again, Joanne saw it was up to her to push the conversation forward. "Where *is* Henry?" she asked.

Joanne felt a prickling sensation creep over the surface of her skin.

She caught Elena's eye.

Saw her fear.

Finally, Stephen Foldes replied, saying, "You have no need to worry. The problem has been taken care of ... The *Foldes* will soon leave this house. No longer shall we burden Goonherth Bay."

Joanne realised it was now or never.

She and Elena had to move.

Or *die*.

ELENA
8.46 PM, SUNDAY

Elena was first off the mark.

As if she read Joanne's mind.

She grabbed hold of Joanne's hand and the two of them bolted from the room.

Elena expected to find Edward and Jock hot on their heels.

But she heard no sound of pursuit.

Still holding onto Joanne's forearm, she steered her through the corridors of the house. She could still hear the *babble* of laughter coming from the drawing room.

She had no urge to go in there ... even if it was to warn the others.

This was survival now.

She and Joanne had to get away.

And *fast*.

When Elena arrived at the front door, she busted the latch down.

She glanced back at Joanne.

Saw she was looking over her shoulder.

The front door swung open.

Elena and Joanne pounded down the steps.

Joanne stumbled a couple of times, but Elena kept her on her feet.

She was determined to keep her friend safe from danger.

The gravel driveway crunched beneath their feet.

Elena looked to the half dozen or so cars sitting in the driveway.

And realised they didn't have the keys for *any* of them.

Their bikes weren't an option either.

Joanne's was still at school and Elena's had been damaged earlier.

Again, as if reading her mind, Joanne said, "Doesn't matter! Let's *go!*"

Elena wasn't about to argue.

As the two of them bounded down the gravel driveway, Elena noted it had stopped raining. The clouds continued to lurk overhead, however. Every couple of minutes moonbeams fanned through. Illuminating the world in a half-light.

It took an almost impossibly long time to get a good distance from The Crosses and even then Elena couldn't allow herself to feel it was a *safe* distance.

She was nearly unaware of the picturesque image of Goonherth Bay to their side.

Despite having grown up here, she never tired of looking out across the water.

Of *imagining* what might be on the other side of the sea.

As they neared the gate at the bottom of the driveway, Joanne took the lead.

She injected fresh pace.

Much-needed extra pace.

As Elena struggled to keep up, she shifted one final glare over her shoulder at the house on the hill.

The Crosses.

A few steps later, the house slipped behind a bush.

Hidden.

Her heart thumped hard in her throat and she squeezed Joanne's hand tighter.

They slowed to a gentle jog as they progressed over the public road leading away from The Crosses. The immediate danger was gone. With each step they took, they were fractionally closer to safety.

It was then that Elena thought she heard coughing.

A *spluttering, whooping* cough.

She stopped and turned to look.

Joanne arrived beside her almost instantly.

Grabbed her arm.

Urged her onward.

But Elena stood her ground.

"Who's there?!"

The moon slipped behind a cloud and everything fell into darkness.

There was a stirring in the ditch at the side of the road.

A voice responded.

"... It's me."

"Henry?" Elena said. "Is that you?"

She tried to move in the direction of the voice but Joanne held her firm, stopping her going any further.

Elena turned into her. "What's wrong?"

Joanne's expression contorted. "I told myself it was over — that there would be no more Henry Foldes."

"We can't just *leave* him here!"

Joanne said nothing in reply.

Finally, Elena summoned the strength to shake off Joanne's hold. Although Joanne didn't make to follow Elena, neither did she try to stop her advancing into the darkness.

In the direction of Henry's voice.

"Henry?" Elena said, conscious of keeping her voice low.

Could she hear the *crunch* of gravel?

Over her shoulder, a car engine trundled into life.

And another.

Another still.

Guests leaving the house ... guests who were tired of the party.

Or ... but that didn't bear thinking about.

Elena almost tripped over Henry's crumpled form.

When she crouched down, she felt the damp grass against her calves.

She felt for his hands.

When their skin made contact, it was an eerie sensation.

Like cold porridge.

Realising she didn't have the strength to lift Henry, she turned around and looked to Joanne. "Please! I need your help!"

Joanne continued to stand in the middle of the road.

And then, with the sound of gravel crunching beneath tyres growing ever-louder — and the *roar* of the engines beginning to rumble through the ground beneath their feet — Joanne lurched into action.

Confusion reigned as Joanne charged into Elena's midriff, sending her tumbling through the air. Elena was aware of her body falling into the ditch.

She landed flat on her back.

The damp earth softened her fall.

On her back, she stared up at the sky.

At a rare cloudless patch showcasing stars.

A little moonlight too.

As the engines became impossibly loud, Elena held herself very still.

As did Joanne and Henry who she realised were lying beside her.

The cars trundled along slowly.

Picking their way over the public road.

Headed toward Goonherth Village.

Headlights shone brightly above their heads. Vibrations rushed through the ground with the force of an earthquake. The fresh, clean, smell of rain which had hung in the air was replaced by the stink of exhaust fumes. As the cars passed them by, that same exhaust washed in over the lip of the ditch, drowning them in its smog.

Elena didn't dare move a muscle until the car engines had disappeared into the distance, replaced by the faint shushing of the tides in Goonherth Bay below.

"We have to go," Elena said to Joanne.

She looked to Henry.

He was lying very still.

There was a smell similar to the damp earth but sharper.

More pungent.

Blood.

"He's injured," Elena said, trying not to let the panic enter her tone of voice. "It'll need both of us to lift him. We have to get him to the village, get him to hospital."

Elena could've dialled an ambulance using her mobile phone ordinarily, but not up here, not up on the hill. It was a notorious signal-free spot.

Henry said something.

It was impossible to understand anything but mumbling.

In the gloom, Elena could make out the dark patch on his shirt.

Where blood seeped through.

He clutched his hands to the spot and Elena realised he was applying pressure to his wound. Preventing the bleeding as best he could.

Unsure quite what to do with this information, she looked to Joanne who was looking off along the road as if expecting the cars to return.

There was no sign of headlights now, though.

Henry sucked in a mouthful of air and did his best to speak in his shaky voice.

"He ... *knows* ... where ... where ... *live.*"

"Who?" Elena replied. "Where *who* lives?"

Afflicted by the constant pain sawing through him, Henry winced.

Momentarily, he appeared to get his thoughts straighter.

He eyed Elena.

"Where you live." He nodded in Joanne's direction. "Where *you* live."

Panic shot through Elena.

Her blood thrummed about her veins.

She thought of her mother.

And she thought of her baby.

... There was Joanne's sister, and her children, too, of course.

"Then we have to go now," Elena said, somehow managing to keep her head clear, finding the presence of mind to make decisions.

Henry shook his head. "No ... *no* ... they don't *want* ... they want ... they want ..."

"*You?*" Elena said, butting in.

Henry nodded, drawing shuddering breaths. "We have to ... we *must* go back."

"Where?" Elena replied, beginning to tremble.

"To the house."

Elena looked to Joanne, and then back to Henry.

It seemed he wasn't quite finished.

"There are some ... some supplies ... *enough* ... for me."

Elena looked over the road.

She considered their options.

They could simply ignore Henry, of course.

They could just leave him here.

They could return to their respective homes.

But what would become of them?

If it was as Henry said, and the others — Edward, Jock, Henry's father — were only searching for Henry, then they would have no trouble. But it was also clear that if they didn't get Henry some proper medical supplies — some proper medical *attention* — he might die within hours. Minutes, perhaps?

Then there was the question of whether they found Henry.

They would surely kill him if they did.

Finish off the job.

And if he did die it would be Elena's responsibility.

Her fault.

How would she feel about that?

She turned the thought over for a few seconds.

Considered what he had done, all those years ago ... and yet if she let him die she would be no better. Worse, she would be *just like him*.

Or just like he *had* been.

She looked at him again and then glanced at Joanne.

Tried to get a read on her mind.

"I don't know," Joanne replied. "I don't *know* if I can."

A rush of anger ploughed through Elena. "Fine," she said, reaching for Henry.

Somehow, she managed to get him up on his feet.

Joanne, too, rose.

Elena draped her arm over Henry's shoulder and the two of them clambered up the side of the ditch. She didn't look at Joanne again until The Crosses came into view.

When she did, Joanne was gone.

Elena cursed to herself.

So much for friendship ... some people never changed.

With Henry dragging her down, she proceeded up the winding gravel driveway.

JOCK

9.02 PM, SUNDAY

J ock lurked in the shadows of the front hall.

He had decided *he* would stay behind.

After all, he was only a Johnny-come-lately.

He really knew nothing about how things worked.

It had seemed only natural to allow Edward and Stephen Foldes to take the car.

And for him to hold the fort here.

He thought back to how he had gone upstairs, soon after Elena and Joanne had fled the music room. It'd been nothing more than a whim. He had slipped the key into the lock of the bedroom door, turned it, then peered inside.

Henry's mother hadn't changed from before, of course.

Silent.

Dead.

But when Jock had shifted to look at where he had left Henry bleeding to death, he had seen nothing but the drying blood on the floorboards; the bloody handprints on the walls. Those trails had led him over to the open window — the source of the fierce chill which snapped about the room. He had peered outside.

To the drainpipe.

The cliché of it all had nearly made him smile.

Nearly.

He had glanced off across the grounds, tried his best to spot the departing Henry Foldes, but he had seen no trace of him. Jock had advised Edward and Stephen Foldes of the development. They had taken the car, going in search of Henry.

Jock recalled how he had stayed close to Stephen Foldes as he had dismissed the last few people attending the party. As Stephen had told them that it was time to *go*.

Minds dulled by alcohol, and by onrushing memories of their "school days", they had all risen and gone to their cars.

One by one, they had driven off.

With Edward and Stephen Foldes among them.

As Jock stood in the shadows of the front hall, he thought about the sounds of the last of the party-goers treading the gravel driveway.

Car doors screeching open, slamming shut.

He could no longer hear the engines.

They had *long* gone.

But he *could* hear the sound of the gravel driveway crunching.

And it was getting louder.

Someone approaching the house by foot.

Jock reached inside his jacket, producing the flick knife.

He had inherited the knife from Max.

After he had killed him.

Max had made his decision when he had turned down the opportunity to join him and Edward in obtaining "justice". When he and Edward had slit Max's throat and left him for dead within one of the toilet cubicles at school, he and Edward had proceeded to "take care" of Mr Blindfield. Jock couldn't help believing that in some way Max was *part* of him now ... they were joined as one.

And now it fell to Jock to finish things.

To *finally* take their revenge.

To kill the one who had caused so much misery.
Jock focused on the front door, waiting for it to open.
How far away were they?
... Thirty seconds, twenty seconds?
Jock thought he could already smell blood.

JOANNE

9.04 PM, SUNDAY

To Joanne, last night seemed like such a long time ago.

As if her embraces with Henry had happened in a past life.

As if the reality in which those things had taken place was an alternate one.

Here she was, freezing cold, clutching her arms across her chest as she trod her way back to the village, doing her best to ward away the chill.

And with such a beautiful view down on Goonherth Bay.

A view like that was wasted on her.

It always had been.

Joanne sensed the shifting of terrain beneath her feet.

She had hit asphalt, so different from the rocky worn-down road which led up to The Crosses. Finding the road in the dark was an achievement in itself. She sighed out hard, some of the tension in her shoulders unknotting. With the next few steps, however, continuing to tread her way back to the village, something niggled away at the back of her mind.

Regret?

Was it because she'd left Elena behind?

Because she'd left Elena to attend to the wounded Henry?

Why *did* Joanne feel as if there was something which connected the two of them?

Why *did* she feel that she had any sort of *responsibility* for him?

Was it some mothering instinct nagging her that she could do something more?

It was easy to reason away fleeing The Crosses.

It was for her own safety.

For her children's safety.

All the same, she couldn't quite shake the idea that Elena had stayed. She had overcome whatever compelled her to seek out her own safety.

But then hadn't Henry guaranteed their safety?

Could Joanne really abide by such assurances?

Without consciously thinking about it, Joanne's walking pace slowed.

And then she stopped completely.

She glanced around, as if someone might leap out of the bushes.

But there was no one, of course.

This was her decision.

What else could she do?

HENRY

9.06 PM, SUNDAY

Despite everything — despite the extreme *pain* — Harry felt slighted that he had to rely on Elena. That he had to *trust* her to aid him up the gravel driveway.

She was much stronger than he would've given her credit for.

And the fact she didn't have Joanne to help only made the feat more impressive.

Joanne had stayed — back there.

Back on the public road leading away from The Crosses ...

And Henry had been so sure she would've helped him.

If anybody had decided to flee he would've thought it would be Elena.

What *reason* did Elena have to help *him?*

Especially when her own safety was on the line.

Although Harry had felt confident in his assurance that neither Joanne nor Elena would come to any harm by the hands of Edward or his father, doubts began to creep in.

How could he tell for certain *exactly* how any given person was feeling?

Who was he to make such a claim after what they had done?

He was woozy from the blood loss. It was affecting his sense of judgement.

As Harry eyed the front door, he couldn't help but think of Christmas, when there would be a wreath hanging there:

Holly, tinsel, red ribbon.

His mother had always taken extreme pride in Christmas decorations.

It was difficult to believe she was dead.

In fact, his brain refused to acknowledge the fact ...

Elena helped him clamber up the steps to the front door and then she reached out and turned the handle. The door wasn't locked. When the door swung back, however, Harry did see that all the lights were off.

Entering The Crosses was like being plunged into a coal mine.

Dead, damp, earthy, woody.

Henry said nothing.

Because he had just crossed eyes with a familiar face.

Emerging from the shadows.

Jock Jones.

ELENA

9.09 PM, SUNDAY

Elena took in Jock Jones.

And the knife he held down at his side.

Exhaustion hardly gave her a moment to think.

It had been an arduous task helping Henry up the gravel driveway, back up to The Crosses and her body ached all over. It seemed as if even her *blood* had become heavier.

Her very *essence* weighed her down.

Feeling Jock's gaze upon her, she lugged Henry on, into the kitchen. She set him down in one of the chairs, aware that Jock was calmly following on her heels, watching each and every move.

A sense of annoyance struck her.

She looked back over her shoulder, caught Jock's eye.

"Are you going to stand there, or are you going to *help?*"

Jock smirked slightly. "Let me put him out of his misery."

Elena didn't pause to analyse his words. "If you want to get to him you'll have to go through me first."

Jock said nothing in reply.

She spotted the phone across the kitchen, resting on its cradle.

Following her gaze — and apparently her line of thought — Jock said, "I've already disconnected the phones. Even if you did call we are out in the boonies. Be lucky if they turn up tomorrow morning."

Unable to prevent herself from matching the sneering tone of Jock's voice, Elena found herself replying, "Maybe if I say that some-one's had their throat slit they'll send a helicopter."

Jock shrugged, smirked some more.

He seemed to enjoy having got a rise out of her.

"Guess we'll never know."

Elena was glad to allow the conversation to drift into silence.

She busied herself with Henry, looking over his wound.

The wound had begun to scab, although blood continued to ooze out around the edges. This needed a professional ... but she was the best Henry had for now.

Straightening up, Elena looked Jock in the eye. "Will you let me out — to go and fetch some medical supplies?"

Jock's expression was neutral now. "You can go," he replied, "but there's no guarantee he'll still be alive when you return."

Elena looked to Henry.

He was stone-faced ... utterly unmoved by what Jock had said.

Maybe he was in so much pain he no longer cared.

Or maybe there was something more there.

Did Henry refuse to believe that Jock Jones — the weedy weirdo from school — could truly do him any serious harm? Perhaps on any normal day that might have been true and Henry wouldn't have had any trouble beating Jock into a pulp.

But today wasn't a normal day.

Elena remained where she was.

She couldn't leave Henry behind.

She wouldn't just let someone die no matter who it was.

And so they were locked in a stalemate.

Deeply aware of Jock's watchful gaze, Elena opened and shut cupboards, hoping she might find *something*. She was on the cusp of turning to ask Henry whether his father kept a first-aid kit in the kitchen when something caught her eye.

She wasn't certain why ... perhaps it was the quaint moleskin cover.

Silver-lined pages.

Whatever it was, she couldn't help but reach out for the book.

She took it in her hands, flipped through the pages.

It was filled with tightly coiled handwriting.

All written out in black ink.

She turned back to the first page.

A *contents* page.

She looked down the list of names.

Her heart quickened as she took in each one.

The names were written in a random order, not listed by either given name or the first name. She found her own name about three quarters of the way down the second page: Elena Kardos.

When she glanced up, to Jock standing in the kitchen doorway, to Henry, face wrinkled in pain, slumped in one of the chairs, they both fixed their attention on her.

Henry was first to speak. "It's *his* book," he said. "*Dad's* book ..."

When Henry squeezed his eyes together, clearly suffering a fresh bout of stinging discomfort, Elena decided to ask further questions.

"The names?" she said. "They read like a register of our school year at Saint Camelgal's." She paused and then added, feeling a little dopey, "But they're written out of order ..."

Henry winced through the pain. "No," he said, "they're ... *in* order."

Elena turned back to the book, looked over the names again.

And then it struck her.

"They're written in the order that your father met these people?"

Henry smiled back before grimacing with pain.

Curious — if that was the right word — Elena flipped the pages through to her entry. An entire page dedicated to her.

Her surname.

Date of birth.

Parents' names.

... Her *child's* name.

The latest entry was from about a week ago.

All it simply said was:

Shopping in the supermarket with George.

A chill crept up her spine.

Henry's *father* had been watching her.

She turned the pages.

Henry's father had been watching *everyone*.

Elena returned to her page.

Something else caught her eye.

For one of the entries near the top of the page Henry's father had written a date Elena recognised. A date that would forever remained scarred into her mind.

The day she had slept with Henry.

Beside the date was a single word:

Scarred.

A tingle ran down her inner thigh.

Where Henry had cut her.

She turned her attention onto Henry.

And he looked back at her.

They seemed to understand what was on one another's mind.

He met her eye.

She noticed that tears ran down his cheeks.

It stunned her.

Were they tears of pain ... or regret?

Elena turned the page in the journal.

And her stomach sank.

A sketch of her sleeping posture in profile.

The drawing was detailed.

As she examined the sketch further, she saw that the artist — if that was the right word to use — had cropped out Henry from the image.

When had Stephen Foldes come? When had he snuck into the room?

He had clearly done it before she had been cut.

On instinct, Elena looked to Jock.

"Do you see?" Jock said. "Do you *understand?* It was systematic. There was more to it than just *off-the-cuff* nastiness. It was planned — *all* planned."

Elena still wasn't quite sure what she made of this.

The question which kept coming back to her was ... *Why?*

"Now's our chance," Jock said. "We can make it *right.*"

Elena frowned. "Would killing him really make things right?"

"Think about all of the lives he destroyed by doing what he did ... by carrying out the acts that he did."

Elena still couldn't bring herself to fall down on either side. It was one thing to think of that which'd taken place in her past, and it was another to feel that she should continue to feel slighted by it — that she should feel *driven* to seek out revenge.

Just what had she been thinking when she'd called Jock and Max to her house?

Just *what* had she been thinking floating that notion of "revenge"?

What was she thinking now?

Finally, Henry spoke up.

"It was him — it was *all* him."

He paused for a long moment.

When he spoke again, his voice was rasping, nearly broken.

"My father."

STEPHEN

9.15 PM, SUNDAY

S tephen Foldes clenched the steering wheel as he turned the tightly wound corners of Goonherth Village.

A few specks of rain fell upon the windshield.

He tapped the wipers on ... watched the raindrops smear across the glass.

Edward sat beside him, leaning forward in his seat, fingers splayed across the dashboard. His eyes were intent. He was *determined* to scope out something or other.

He was determined to be the one to make the breakthrough.

Stephen, though, had come to the conclusion that there wasn't any breakthrough to be made. To be sure, they would keep on going along the path they had travelled so far. They had already visited Joanne Darkly's house, and found no trace of Henry there. Next they would stop by Elena's house, on the way back to The Crosses.

There was a chance — Stephen supposed — that Henry might've ended up there.

Stephen had banked on finding Henry near Joanne ... it had always been obvious to him just how highly his son *prized* her. But there had been no sign.

He brought the car to a halt outside Elena Kardos's house.

He glanced briefly to Edward, and then stepped out of the car.

Into the breeze which blew in over the bay.

He paused briefly, considering the ocean.

Every morning, when he woke, he would put on a pot of coffee and sit in the drawing room, admiring the sea. It had a calming effect on him.

It preserved his sanity.

It reminded him he was *still* part of the world ... however hard he might try to separate himself from it.

When Edward made a move to slip out of the passenger seat and join him outside the car, Stephen gave him the merest shake of the head. And Edward stayed put.

Some things required tact.

Subtlety.

Edward had learned that lesson a long time ago — early in his music career.

He couldn't use the same tools for every composition and performance.

He needed to pick and choose ... and, of course, constantly reinvent.

Stephen trod up to Elena's front door.

He recalled, from his journal, that this was her mother's house.

She'd moved back to Goonherth Village about a year ago with a baby.

No sign of a father.

Not that such a thing was atypical these days.

Modern times. Modern families.

To each their own.

When Stephen knocked on the door, he expected Elena to appear.

However it was an older woman.

Elena's mother.

It frustrated him that he couldn't immediately recall her name.

Sometimes these things just slipped his mind ... that was why he kept a journal.

He asked after Elena.

She told him she wasn't there.

Elena's mother had a thick foreign accent, although her English was fluent. It reminded him of his tours throughout Europe; the many varied versions of English which would greet him in each place.

When Stephen heard a baby crying off in the depths of the house, he wondered if she was telling the truth. Was Elena's mother covering for her? Had Elena told her not to respond to strangers calling in the middle of the night?

When Elena's mother wished him a pleasant evening and closed the door in his face, Stephen remained standing there for about a minute.

He wanted to *listen* ... he wanted to *ensure* he hadn't missed anything ...

He got the impression that he had somehow been swindled.

That his dear son had succeeded in evading detection.

But, if he had, there was only one place he would be now.

Stephen turned back to the car — back to Edward.

He got back in, asked Edward if he had seen any cars driving by as he had been speaking to Elena's mother. Edward shook his head.

Although Stephen had been sure he hadn't heard anything — he had only been standing on the doorstep a few paces away, after all — it never hurt to have his suspicions confirmed.

He turned the key in the ignition and fired up the engine.

JOANNE
9.22 PM, SUNDAY

T he house was eerily silent.

Perhaps this was its normal state.

Joanne recalled the previous night, when she had come to Henry, when she had dropped in to visit. She couldn't remember the house seeming so silent then ...

She was aware of the sound her footsteps might make over the gravel driveway, so she had taken to walking along the grass. This allowed her a silent approach to the house. Besides the light from the front hall, the house was plunged into darkness.

She had a great urge to turn around.

To go home.

But a similar urge had implored she return.

And now here she was.

She wouldn't *run*.

She rounded the house and went in through a back door.

She heard no voices.

Even though it was impossible, she thought she could sense body heat clamouring through the air. She trod along, sensing some people in the kitchen.

When she noticed the figure standing in the doorway, she froze.

It was Jock.

He had his back to her.

And all this time they had believed that the three of them — Edward, Jock and Henry's father — had left the house behind!

Joanne never thought of herself as a violent person, but she saw no other way.

It wasn't a matter of making a decision.

The decision had already been made.

She rushed at Jock, elbow outstretched.

Caught him in the lower back.

He tumbled to the kitchen floor.

She dived on top of him.

Held her weight on him.

Jock scrabbled for her.

But he could get no purchase.

Joanne supposed it was a good thing she hadn't shed *all* of her pregnancy weight.

It was only when she looked to Elena's face, and then to Henry, that she realised the implications of what she had done. She had broken the deadlock ... she was "the cat among the pigeons".

"The knife!" Elena said. "*Grab* it!"

Joanne looked about her, saw a flick knife, flipped open, lying on the floor.

Jock was attempting to make a grab for it.

He wanted to *stab* her.

He wanted to *kill* her.

Keeping one eye on Jock, Joanne reached for the knife.

She grabbed it at her first effort.

Snapped it shut.

Realising Jock was trying to get some momentum into his legs, that he wanted to thrust her off him, swing back onto his feet, Joanne shifted her weight onto his chest.

She was only satisfied when she had him pinned.

When he had no hope of getting back up.

This victory was short-lived, however, because both Elena and Henry looked off in the direction of the driveway.

Joanne soon realised why.

A car.

They could hear a *car* approaching.

Joanne looked to Elena, unable to get the question out before Elena answered.

"Upstairs!" Elena said, already rushing to grab hold of Henry.

Joanne vaguely wondered what she should do with Jock, but, when she felt him get his arms free, and grab for her throat, it was only a natural instinct for her to punch him square in the forehead.

His head snapped back.

Made contact with the kitchen floor.

His eyelids flickered a few times, and then closed tight.

Knocked out.

Joanne experimented, shifting her weight off him.

She eased herself back up onto her feet.

She stared down at Jock, daring him to move a muscle.

To reveal that he wasn't in the Land of Dreams.

He seemed out cold.

"Quickly!" Elena called, now out in the hall, headed up the staircase.

Somewhat reluctantly, Joanne eased herself up off Jock.

She didn't dare turn her back, keeping an eye on him as she retreated for the staircase. It surprised her to see that Elena, propping up Henry beside her, was already halfway to the next floor.

Outside, Joanne heard a pair of car doors slamming.

The sound might as well have been gunshots.

STEPHEN
9.26 PM, SUNDAY

S tephen left the car behind.

He ventured in through the front door.

He never saw any reason to lock the front door, not in a place like Goonherth Bay, where the grimmest of crimes tended to be lost dogs or misplaced property.

The front hall was quiet.

Light trickled in from the kitchen.

With Edward on his heels, he turned to look.

And took in the prostate body.

Jock.

At first, Stephen was convinced he must be dead, but as he trod closer, he could tell he was still breathing — that his chest continued to rise and fall.

He paused to look briefly and then looked through the kitchen doorway.

At the kitchen counter.

He saw his journal.

Even without getting any closer, he could tell someone had opened it.

Without fail, after consulting his journal, he always plucked a hair from his head and — with the tiniest globs of spit — he would paste it between the two covers. The system was simple: if the hair remained it meant his journal had been left without being disturbed. However, if the hair had been broken, or had been otherwise displaced, then the journal had been consulted.

And without his permission.

Stephen never felt anger, much less rage.

And neither was he someone who was particular about their possessions.

He didn't much mind whether people touched his piano, or if they left fingerprints on the many framed posters hanging in the music room. However what *did* tend to get on his nerves was people wading into his personal space.

And especially when they attempted to get inside his mind.

"Do you think they're still here?" Edward asked.

In observing that his journal had been disturbed, Stephen had almost forgotten Edward was there. He glanced back, managed to put on a smile. "Yes," he replied. "They're still here — *Henry's* still here."

With that, Stephen turned away from the spread-eagled Jock, turning his attention onto the front hall, and the staircase which led to the upper floors. As he was on the brink of leaving the kitchen behind, Edward spoke up again.

"Do we leave him here — on the floor?"

"Yes," Stephen replied. "Leave him."

The two of them ventured into the front hall.

And up the stairs.

ELENA

9.29 PM, SUNDAY

Once upstairs, Elena could feel Henry's breathing coming shallow.

A couple of times she had felt the giveaway sensation of dead weight up against her shoulder. She was glad Joanne was there to help her out.

That she had taken some of the weight off her.

In the end, they had ventured into one of the many rooms off the landing, unable to get any sort of a comprehendible response out of Henry.

An idea for a hiding place.

The room they settled upon smelled strongly.

Even as they crossed the threshold it was an overpowering odour.

But, already, Elena had heard the front door open and shut.

She knew there was no time.

That they had to hide.

Since they hadn't flipped on the lights, the only light source came from the moonlight streaming down over Goonherth Bay. Elena could make out the faint outline of someone lying on the bed — *sleeping* — their silhouette against the window.

There was a wardrobe, and then a smaller door to the further reaches of the room.

Not really thinking, acting out of basic survival instinct, Elena led the others toward the door. It had no lock on it. Elena butted her hip hard against it to get it open.

She peered inside.

It was some sort of closet.

Small, but large enough to accommodate them.

There was also a duvet stuffed in there.

She glanced at Joanne and Henry, hoping she might receive some guidance.

But neither seemed interested in handing out counsel.

Elena heard the creaking of floorboards close by.

Too close.

There was nowhere else for them to go.

Nowhere else for them to *hide.*

So she ducked down and, with Joanne's assistance, eased Henry's head in beneath the doorframe. The space was both narrower and longer than Elena had anticipated.

Henry became more lucid as she eased him in. His limbs went slack and his arms fell flush with his sides. Before long, Elena had him slotted into place.

Joanne was next.

She slid in there without trouble.

That left only Elena.

She could hear floorboards creaking just outside the door now.

She looked back to the closet where Henry and Joanne were concealed.

Then she made her decision.

With Joanne's eyes glued to her own, she brought the door shut.

Sealing Joanne and Henry inside.

Elena straightened up, turned and faced the door leading into the room.

Listened to the whispering voices outside.
A second later the door opened.
And two figures appeared in the doorway.
Stephen Foldes.
Edward Wanton.

STEPHEN

9.33 PM, SUNDAY

S tephen stood in the doorway of the guest room.

It was the room he kept in clean sheets and good order.

Ready for unexpected visitors.

In the past decade, the room had only been used a handful of times.

Now, though, it seemed to be getting a *good deal* of use.

He looked to the girl standing before him.

Elena Kardos.

Behind her, he could make out someone lying on the bed.

To begin with, Stephen believed it to be Joanne Darkly, lying down, taking a rest. But, he decided, from what he had memorised of her figure — of her *posture* while sleeping — that it couldn't be her ... It *was* a body he was familiar with though.

And then it came to him.

Jasmine Everglade.

He thought she had gone home hours ago.

Apparently not.

Stephen thought back to his journal. He had sketched many

sleeping postures among those pages, including Elena's. Had Elena flipped through the pages and come across her outline?

Stephen could feel Edward's warm breath against the nape of his neck.

Here was Elena, but what about the others?

Where was his son?

Henry.

As if he had sent him some silent order, Edward left him, treading off along the landing. Stephen let him go. There could be no harm in him searching the house. It would be *extremely* problematic if his son succeeded in escaping the house.

Stephen managed a smile. "You rushed off before I got a chance to finish."

Elena remained still.

He noticed her eyelid twitch.

"The only one we want is *Henry*," he said. "You're free to go." He paused. "You *and* Joanne, if she's still here."

Since Elena appeared unmoved by this declaration — as if she didn't believe him — he stood to one side so he no longer blocked the doorway. He gestured to the space behind him. "Go on. Everyone else has gone home. The party is winding down."

But Elena still didn't move.

Finally, she spoke.

"Why do you keep that journal?" she asked.

"Oh," he replied, brushing away an invisible piece of lint on his shirt sleeve, "a *silly* thing — just something my therapist recommended."

"Your 'therapist'?"

Stephen had never had a therapist, of course, but Elena didn't need to know that.

"Yes," Stephen replied. "You see, I decided to come here — to bring my *family* here — when I was diagnosed with a nervous disposition." He smiled, hoping to make the story more convincing. "My therapist thought I would be able to get a better hold on my surroundings — on my *own* world — if I created an encyclopaedia of those close to me."

"I was never close to you," Elena replied, her lips thin, complexion pallid.

"You can never imagine how *close* this village is to me — and all the people who reside in it." He flashed his eyebrows, highlighting the fact that Elena was free to go.

Elena apparently didn't register the hint.

Or she didn't want to leave.

"You're going to kill him, aren't you?" she said.

Stephen felt his chest tighten.

He said nothing in reply.

And made sure not to react in any way.

"Whatever brought that thought into your mind?"

Elena remained silent.

She seemed almost divine with the moonlight shining behind her.

As if she was standing upon a stage.

It whipped Stephen back momentarily to his theatrical days.

Deciding the only way to get shot of Elena, without complications, would be for him to be direct with her, he said, "Some might call it justice."

" 'Justice' ?"

Here Stephen couldn't help smiling. "Surely you've heard about what Henry — *my son* — did? Surely you have heard about the castrations? You yourself experienced his brutality first-hand. Did you not?"

Elena flinched.

Stephen could tell he was getting to her now.

Good.

Perhaps she would go.

Now he needed to up the ante.

"Leave, Elena. Forget about this. Forget about The Crosses. Forget about the Foldeses. You shall have that which is rightfully yours."

Elena remained standing where she was.

Then she looked off, over Stephen's shoulder.

Finally she slipped past him and out the door.

Stephen stood where he was, listening to her footsteps disappearing off through the house. The creaking of floorboards. When the footsteps finally faded into silence, he took one final look around the room before fixing his gaze on the sleeping Jasmine.

Satisfied Henry wasn't in the room, he turned around and ventured out.

Perhaps Edward had had better luck.

ELENA
9.34 PM, SUNDAY

Elena left the guest room behind.

The house felt impossibly large.

She reached out her arm and brushed the wallpaper with her fingertips as she passed by. She thought back to Joanne, and to Henry, the two of them hidden away in that closet. She had succeeded in distracting Stephen.

She had bought them time.

What they chose to do with that time was another matter entirely ...

As she descended the stairs, she kept a careful watch on her surroundings.

She was alert to the possibility of someone sneaking up on her.

She couldn't shake the idea that Stephen Foldes had deceived her somehow.

That he had only turned her loose so Edward would take her prisoner.

When Elena reached the bottom of the staircase, she kept her eyes fixed on the front door. The latch which she would need to shove down.

Soon she would be *outside* ... running down the driveway ... returning *home.*

Stephen Foldes had said that he had no intention of causing her harm.

That this was nothing to do with her.

And what other option did she have but to believe him?

Right as she got to the front door, she looked over her shoulder.

Through the kitchen doorway.

To where Jock had lain on the floor.

When Joanne had knocked him flat.

He wasn't *there.*

When she craned her neck to get a better look, she felt warm breath against the side of her neck. When she turned, she was staring into Jock's wide eyes.

Elena had no time to do anything other than feel the *bump* on her head.

HENRY

9.38 PM, SUNDAY

Henry's whole body was in shock as he lay beside Joanne.
He listened to his father's footsteps become quieter.

The guest room door shutting behind him.

Henry felt so hot he was having trouble breathing.

Sweat soaked him.

His clothes clung to his skin.

And he was experiencing an apparently unstoppable pain.

The feeling that Jock had cut him open to bleed him out.

Henry took short, sharp breaths, trying to stay conscious.

Above all else, he wanted to protect Joanne ... even as he thought it, Henry knew it was ridiculous to believe he would be able to protect her in his current state.

Elena had left.

Had she gone to call for help?

Even if she had, Henry didn't believe it would arrive in time.

Joanne jostled beside him. "I ... can ... hardly ... *breathe*," she said.

Although Henry couldn't find the strength to reply, he shared the sensation.

He wanted nothing more than to spring from their hiding place.

To stand up straight and draw deep breaths down into his lungs.

And then he could think about the pain again.

Then he could allow his mind to think about how he might *deal* with the pain.

But all there was for the time being was their shallow breathing.

And the heat.

"It's true, isn't it?" Joanne said, in a husky whisper. "What your father said ... about those castrations ... about the *mutilations* ... ?"

Henry allowed her words to swill about his mind. In the end, it was as much his exasperation as his will to tell the truth which led to his response.

"Yes."

There was a long silence between them.

Henry felt clammy all over.

His heart beat slow and weak.

He wondered if he might be close to passing out.

He might be drawing his last breaths.

This could be his final opportunity to tell the *full* story.

So, with that revelation, he sucked up his strength, directing his words at Joanne. "She ... *knew*."

"Who knew?"

Henry breathed in through his nostrils, hoping he might somehow mitigate the pain. But it only made the pain worse. He caught his breath. "My ... *mother* ..."

Henry felt Joanne go still beside him. He could tell she was attempting to get her head around what he had just told her. He knew he had to keep going.

Or else the truth would never be known.

"He ... *did* something ... something to her ..."

"What?" Joanne replied, her voice more insistent now. "*What* did he do?"

"I ... she's ... gone ... *dead*."

Again, Henry sensed Joanne taking in this news, turning it over in her mind, trying to get a hold on just what he was telling her. He straightened his thoughts out, then added, "*He* killed her ... to bring ... to *bring* me ... *here*."

"For the reunion?"

Henry attempted a smile, but it only came across as a wince.

It didn't matter anyway in the darkness.

Joanne couldn't see him.

"Edward ... here ... he ..."

Henry could feel himself fading.

Another darkness — more profound even than the one surrounding them — was bleeding in through the periphery of his vision. He knew he could do nothing to prevent it ... this was the *end* ... this was as far as he would go.

And with this revelation fixed in his mind, he reached for Joanne's hand.

Felt her soft skin.

He curled his fingers about hers.

Squeezed one last time.

And simply faded away.

JOANNE

9.44 PM, SUNDAY

There was something about Henry which caught Joanne off guard.

He twitched suddenly.

Then held impossibly still.

Her heart leaped into her throat.

To begin with she couldn't quite believe what'd taken place.

She spoke to him in the darkness.

"Henry? Henry?" She paused. "*Harry?*"

She reached for his wrist.

Felt his pulse.

Nothing.

There was ... *nothing*.

All at once, Joanne had the urge to scream.

But she realised just how foolish that would be.

It would bring Stephen Foldes and Edward back here, to the guest room.

Another thought occurred to Joanne.

She recalled Jasmine.

Sleeping on the bed on the other side of the closet door.

Apparently *oblivious* to what was going on.

Joanne whispered as loudly as she dared, not wanting to push her luck lest she be heard on the landing outside. There was no response. Then again, she supposed that if Stephen Foldes's and Elena's conversation hadn't woken her then her whispers had little chance. And even if Jasmine did wake just what sort of a state would she be in?

She surely wouldn't be *sober* ...

As Joanne felt Henry's cold, dead weight lying beside her, a creeping sensation passed over the surface of her skin.

It sent a shudder down her spine.

She curled her toes.

But forced herself to keep going.

There was no other way.

It was weird to think that only minutes ago she had had no trouble making contact with Henry's skin. Now, though, the very thought of touching him in any way made the hairs rise at the back of her neck.

Something about death was intrinsically *sickening* ...

Joanne got herself into a position to knock open the closet door.

The hinges made a gut-lurching creak as she did so.

She held still.

Looking out into the guest room.

Eyes firmly fixed on the closed door leading to the landing.

Listening closely for any sound.

Edward.

Or Stephen.

The house was silent.

Joanne looked back into the darkness of the closet.

It was difficult to make out more than the vague outline of Henry's body within.

Feeling as if she was thinking a little more logically now, she crouched down, reached out, and pressed her fingers to the side of his neck.

No pulse.

She was sure.

Time for her to leave.

She straightened up, and then, feeling herself thrown by a slight dizzy spell, reached out and steadied herself against the wall.

She turned to the bed, looked over Jasmine's sleeping form.

Joanne drew breath.

The thick stench of blood still hung on the air.

Some smells were impossible to get used to.

Finally, she bent down, considering Jasmine closer.

And it was now that she noticed the blood soaking the mattress.

It was *now* that she realised Jasmine's dress was *covered* in blood.

Her heart rapped at the back of her throat.

And her gut clenched.

She backed away from the body, her hand slowly reaching for her mouth, for her slightly parted lips. All sensible thought had departed her mind when she reached behind her for the door knob.

But found nothing.

Nothing!

Only air.

It was then that she felt something else.

Something *warm*.

A mid-riff.

A body.

A *person*.

Feeling trapped between that which lay within, and that which lay outside, she could do nothing but turn. And take in the person who stood in the doorway.

The person who had soundlessly opened the guest room door.

Edward Wanton.

JOCK

9.49 PM, SUNDAY

J ock had to be quick when he grabbed Elena.

He had brought her to the music room, laid her down on the recliner.

The raised voices upstairs had woken him from where he'd been knocked out on the kitchen floor. When he had reached up to his forehead, he had felt the swelling.

He had felt his heartbeat pounding against his fingertips.

Jock could hear more footsteps now — someone coming downstairs.

He stood.

His mind switching and whirring.

Unsure what to do next.

The first person to walk through the doorway was Edward.

Jock looked over the person he pushed before him.

Joanne.

Joanne *Darkly*.

Jock thought back to the night before, to the "meeting" Elena had called.

When she had floated the possibility of getting *revenge* on Henry Foldes.

He had thought Joanne's presence odd ... she hadn't fit. He understood what she'd been doing there in the end, though, when Elena had ordered her to ensure Henry would show up to the school reunion.

That had been her purpose.

However that purpose had been fulfilled.

Behind Edward, Stephen Foldes walked through the doorway.

Stephen's expression was so neutral, his thoughts so impossible to read, that if Jock hadn't known better he might've believed it was just another day.

That nothing *unusual* had happened.

Edward brought Joanne over to the recliner where Elena lay. Although he held Joanne's wrist tightly, he was clearly taking care not to cause her any unnecessary pain. He offered her the armchair rather than hurling her into it.

Stephen Foldes spoke.

"I apologise for any rough treatment you might have experienced," he said. "But I *would* like to know the location of my son ..."

Joanne broke in. "Your son is *dead!*"

Stephen took this news with an unfocused look, followed by a rapid series of blinks. He looked at Joanne. "Where is he? Where is his *body?*"

Joanne averted his gaze.

She pressed her lips tightly together.

Tilted her head to one side.

Stephen flapped his hand. "It's okay," he said. "If he's in this house I shall find him." He clasped his hands behind his back and strolled back and forth before them, as if turning some elaborate conundrum over in his mind. Finally, he came to a halt. He looked at Joanne. "The two of you may go. Like I said before, neither one of you is involved in this ... you are *free.*"

Jock felt his stomach dip.

It seemed completely the *wrong* thing to do.

And yet Stephen Foldes was in charge.

He padded his jacket pockets, his trouser pockets.

The flick knife wasn't there.

What had he done with it?

He looked over to Elena and Joanne.

Had *they* taken it off him?

Neither Elena or Joanne moved, despite Stephen Foldes's offer for them to leave.

Finally, Joanne spoke. "Henry told me you killed his mother — that you made her *ill* so he would return home. So he would come home for the *reunion*." She looked at Edward, and then, apparently keen to blurt out everything she could, said, "I'll bet you organised this. What was it? Did he promise you your chance to 'get even' with Henry? Your chance to *mutilate* him just like he *mutilated* you?"

Edward's eyes widened.

Jock looked to Stephen Foldes who gave nothing away.

All he said was, "The door is open, girls. Take your leave when it pleases you."

Joanne and Elena exchanged glances.

But neither of them moved.

Stephen drew in a breath, and then sighed out, long and hard. There was something of the performer about him now — emphasised by the tuxedo he wore.

Joanne, however, wasn't finished. "Jasmine is dead, too."

This caught Stephen off guard ... at least he blinked a couple of times.

"She's sleeping," he said. "*Upstairs*."

Joanne gave a snarling grin. "I think you'd better take a closer look — she's *dead*."

Stephen Foldes looked to Edward and then to Jock.

A warmth ran through Jock's blood.

It had been an impulsive killing.

Just like Mr Blindfield and Max Yardsman.

It had just *felt* right.

Stephen Foldes didn't need to know about either. But now, since he knew about one, Jock didn't see the point in concealing the other. "We killed an ex-classmate," Jock said. "And a teacher. Back at the school."

Again, no overt reaction from Stephen Foldes.

He maintained a blank expression.

Finally he muttered under his breath.

"A messy, *messy* business."

"Do you know what I think?"

It was Elena who spoke this time, stirring from the recliner, eyelids droopy.

"I think it was *you* all along — I think *you* wanted to make an impact. Something which would make a *splash* ... something to pass the time."

Jock was certain he saw a shift in Stephen Foldes's posture.

He stood more stiffly now.

With Joanne's help, Elena shifted into a sitting position, rocking her legs around so she sat on the edge of the recliner. She eyeballed Stephen Foldes. "You wanted to *know* you could still keep people captivated — that you could *still* control them. You did that with your son. You did that with *Henry*." She smiled wryly. "That journal, in the kitchen, that was your transcription — the *music* you worked off ... you wanted to see what your son was capable of ... if he could commit these ... these *acts* and get away with them."

She looked to Edward.

"You were his accomplice. Henry used you to achieve his father's goals — and then he turned on you *too* just so there would be no mistake who held the power. Don't you see? He planned this all along. He *wanted* his son to return for the school reunion. This was to be the end of his *piece*. He wanted to watch as you tore one another to pieces; as the two of you" — she fired off a glance in Jock's direction — "tore Henry to pieces."

Edward stood very still now.

He looked at nothing in particular.

He only stared into mid-air.

What was he thinking about?

What was Jock *himself* thinking about?

Before he got the chance to consider matters more closely, Jock blurted out, "I had no agreement — no *plan* with Stephen Foldes."

Jock nodded to Edward.

"Before we met one another in the school toilets today — before we *killed* Max Yardsman — we hadn't spoken more than ten words. It was Edward who suggested it. He asked whether we wanted 'revenge'. And then Max showed us the knife, but said he had no intention of using it ... and all the blood rushed to my head ... I did him *in*."

Those words sounded unnatural coming out of Jock's mouth.

And yet he had only told them what had happened.

The *acts* he had committed.

His *lack* of control.

And yet he was sure about one thing.

"I did it all for *me*," Jock said.

Elena and Joanne both fixed him with their stare.

What else could he say?

He had only told the truth.

Jock could tell that Edward was thinking things over — that he continued to wallow in his wonderings; that he was attempting to get things straight.

Perhaps he felt as if he had been a puppet.

Jock had always believed the popular kids at school, the ones who seemed to exist on another level entirely, were somewhat naive. They thought they were far more unique than they were in reality. That they were far more *original* than they truly were.

But now Edward had had his wake-up call.

Jock couldn't help but feel a shade satisfied.

When he turned his attention onto Elena and Joanne again, he decided one or the other of them had his knife. And he would have it back off them.

Or he would die in the process.

ELENA

9.56 PM, SUNDAY

Elena's head continued to ache.

It felt as if her brain pulsed inside her skull.

She longed to escape from this nightmare.

She *longed* to be gone.

Why had she opened her mouth?

Why had she fixed in her mind that *justice* was something which needed to be done here? Who *cared* what Stephen Foldes was up to? Beyond her appearing in his journals, did it really affect her at all?

She should just go.

Just as Stephen Foldes had *told* her she could.

Did the offer still stand?

There was only one way to know for sure.

Elena rose from the recliner.

She felt everyone's eyes on her.

Stephen's eyes.

Edward's eyes.

Jock's eyes.

Joanne's eyes.

They all wanted to see what she was going to do next.

They all *anticipated* what she was going to do next.

Make for the doorway.

Would any one of them dare to stop her?

Elena took a step forward.

And then another.

Nobody else moved.

She listened for any sound off in the house.

She heard nothing.

She took another step.

Another.

If they did intend to rip one another to pieces they were free to do so.

But she wouldn't be around to see it.

Elena had almost reached the door when she dared to look Edward in the eye.

Why did she look back at all?

Was it just simple curiosity?

Did she just want to know if it was true?

If Edward really *had* been manipulated by Stephen Foldes?

If they had *all* been manipulated by Stephen Foldes?

Just his little *game.*

His *composition.*

And it was then that Edward rushed her.

Elena hardly had time to think.

JOANNE
9.57 PM, SUNDAY

Joanne stood hypnotised by Edward throwing himself at Elena.

She had no time to think.

When she turned, she saw Jock rushing her.

She had no chance to brace herself.

He was far too fast.

Although Jock was hardly a well-built man, the element of surprise, and the force with which he threw himself at her proved sufficient.

She fell to the ground, impulsively throwing out her elbow and catching herself.

Every nerve in her arm jangled as she landed.

As she absorbed the force of her landing.

Before she could reset herself, Jock pinned her to the floor.

His hands moved quickly, padding her down.

He delved into her pocket, uncovering the flick knife she had slipped in there.

She cursed herself for not having hidden it better.

Or having simply discarded it.

What a stupid *bitch*!

Jock flipped the knife open.

With a practised motion, he drew the blade up to her throat.

Her heart stopped beating.

She looked across the room, to Elena.

And to Edward.

He had Elena under his control.

She shifted her attention back to Stephen Foldes.

Felt his gaze move over hers.

As he had been throughout this encounter, he was passive.

Apparently *unmoved*.

The indifferent composer ...

Was there anything she could do to stop him?

Was there *anything* anyone could do to stop him?

STEPHEN
9.58 PM, SUNDAY

Things happened so quickly Stephen hadn't time to act.

He saw him — *Edward* — rush Elena.

Meanwhile Stephen stood his ground.

Waited.

This was the plan.

The most elaborate composition of all.

Everything was falling into place.

It felt so ... *satisfactory*.

Only one detail was missing

One detail had gone awry.

Some critics pushed the case that art could never be perfect, and that was what made it art in the first place. Stephen, though, had always begged to differ.

Because wasn't perfection reached in death?

... And wasn't that ... yes ... he could hear ... coming closer!

... Yes.

Yes!

HENRY

9.59 PM, SUNDAY

Down on the ground, crawling over the bare floorboards, Harry could feel each and every one of his faint, ever-dimming heartbeats.

But he was compelled to keep going.

He had risen from the dead *twice* today.

And he would do so a third time or however many times it took to reach his father.

If he could just get an *answer*.

As he looked into the music room, where he had heard the kerfuffle, he could hardly believe his eyes. The room was alive with motion.

Of limbs and arms.

Elena.

Edward.

Joanne.

Jock.

He could barely keep his eyes open.

But his inner determination fought back against the wooziness.

Against succumbing to the easy option.

Simply slipping away.

Leaving this plane behind ...

But, no ... not yet.

He had unfinished business.

And he refused to leave this world without it being resolved.

Harry focused his attention onto his father.

He towered above it all.

Taking centre stage.

A pair of melees had been taking place.

One between Elena and Edward.

Another between Joanne and Jock.

But both had stopped now.

And all eyes were on him.

It was almost as if Harry was more than himself.

As if he was some sort of symbol.

A *spectacle*.

He eased himself up against the doorframe, steadily straightening.

He took in the others.

And they took *him* in.

Finally, he looked to his father.

Out of nowhere, a smile appeared on his lips.

At first, in his dreary state, Harry took the smile for kindness.

But he soon saw what it really meant.

Or — perhaps more accurately — he realised where he had seen it before.

When he had had homework to do at home, he would often come here to sit in the music room. Exercise book perched on his thigh, he would scribble away.

He had liked to do this.

It meant he could glance up occasionally and look at his father as he sat on the piano stool, playing the odd note or sequence, here and there, writing up compositions on notation paper on the stand. He never handed in these compositions or else performed them. It seemed, at least to Harry, that he composed for his own pleasure.

Because it was who he was.

He couldn't *not* write down the music which entered his mind.

It wasn't a drug, an addiction to his father. It was far more basic than that.

More dangerous.

It was an actual *physical* need ... like breathing or eating.

Without it, quite simply, his father would cease to be.

It was during those times, when his father would take breaks from his music, that he would speak to Harry about school and — more to the point — Harry's *role* there.

At first, when his father had spoken to him about school, Harry had believed that he wanted to *appear* as though he took an interest in his schooling. But his father's interrogations went much further than feigning a passing interest.

His questions were deep, probing.

He would often invite Harry to comment on some aspect of his school day.

Of how Harry *himself* had affected it.

And then his father had started talking about dominance.

About *power*.

And how it should be exercised.

It was during those talks when Harry realised — with the help of several therapists in his adult life — how he had been formed.

How his father had moulded him.

Not in his own image but in the image of *what* he hoped Harry would become.

Although Harry hadn't had the self-awareness to realise it until years later, his father had made him into a *monster*.

His father had manipulated him.

Throughout his childhood.

Until Harry had managed to break free.

And now Harry had returned ... *returned* from death.

To kill him.

His father appeared to understand intuitively what was going to happen.

How things would play out here ... in this final scene.

The others relegated to onlookers.

Witnesses.

Even as Harry trod toward him, he was unsure how it would end.

About how he would *kill* his own father.

But, with each step, it seemed to matter less and less.

He stood only centimetres away from him now.

The tips of their noses almost touched.

Staring into one another's eyes.

Harry felt weak at the knees.

Near to folding in on himself.

But he managed to find the strength to say what he *needed* to say.

"You ... you *killed* her ..."

Just to say those words — and to say them to his father's face — felt as if he had released something ...

Something *deep* within.

It seemed to justify any and all violence which might follow.

If only he could keep himself calm.

If only he could take on the mantle of the *surgeon.*

Cool.

Quick.

Clinical.

Deadly.

In Harry's semi-detached state, he giddily imagined his mind had separated from the rest of his body. He managed to convince himself he was no longer *whole.*

He saw the shock in his father's eyes.

Sensed his father falling toward him.

Falling into his *arms.*

Only as Harry felt his father's weight — felt himself finally buckling at the knees — did he think to look up, to look *beyond.*

He saw him.

Jock Jones.

That boy ... the one from school ... the one he had treated so cruelly.

As Harry fell to the floorboards, no longer able to resist the effect of his injuries, he took in the knife in his father's back, Jock Jones's emotionless face, his cruel, narrowed eyes. There was nothing there which wanted to be sorry.

Why should there be?

The Foldes family name — and the punishment they had meted out — ended here.

ELENA
11.05 PM, MONDAY

Elena stood in the front room of her mother's house.

She was aware of George crying.

Upstairs.

Her mother taking care of him ... trying to *console* him.

She looked to her side.

Saw Joanne standing there.

Like Elena, she hadn't yet changed clothes.

The two of them had looked a state — that much had been apparent from Elena's mother's reaction when they had arrived on the doorstep.

Elena had almost expected her mother to slam the door in their faces.

To let out a shrill, piercing scream.

But, beyond the shock sketching her face, she had remained calm.

It was more than Elena could have asked for.

Much more than Elena could have asked for.

Elena looked to Joanne.

Neither of them had spoken since they had left The Crosses.

They had simply walked silently, side by side, back into Goon-herth Village.

And now they had to contend with what came next.

With what society *compelled* them to do.

What ethics *compelled* them to do.

But most important of all what their instincts *compelled* them to do.

As if it had taken on a symbolism beyond the two of them, Elena turned to Joanne, and said, "I'll call them — the police, I mean ..."

Joanne didn't nod or otherwise respond.

She only stood her ground.

Grave-faced ... as if tempting the world to do her more harm.

To *test* her again.

Elena padded off through her mother's house for the phone.

THE END

AUTHOR'S NOTE

Thank you for taking the time to read one of my books.

I would really appreciate it if you took a moment to leave me a review. Reviews greatly help with visibility on online sales platforms and bring these books to the attention of other readers who might enjoy them!

If you would like to hear about my latest releases you can sign up for my newsletter here: www.aviain.com.

Thanks for reading!

AV Iain

COPYRIGHT INFORMATION

Convenient Prey
A Novel